The Defender

In addition to being a popular and prolific writer for children, Alan Gibbons teaches in a primary school. He is also much in demand as a speaker in schools and at book events. He lives in Liverpool with his wife and four children.

Alan Gibbons has twice been shortlisted for the Carnegie Medal, with *The Edge* and *Shadow of the Minotaur*, which also won the Blue Peter Book Award in the 'Book I Couldn't Put Down' category.

D0058993

The Defender

ALAN GIBBONS

A Dolphin
Paperback

First published in Great Britain in 2004
as a Dolphin paperback
by Orion Children's Books
a division of the Orion Publishing Group Ltd
Orion House
5 Upper St Martin's Lane
London WC2H 9EA

Reprinted 2004

A catalogue record for this book is
available from the British Library

Typeset at The Spartan Press Ltd,
Lymington, Hants

Printed in Great Britain by
Clays Ltd, St Ives plc

ISBN 1 84255 098 5

One

Several people see the men in the green Rover, but only one discovers they are armed. His name is Ian Moore. He is fourteen years old. He doesn't know about them yet, but in just a few minutes he will. Their sudden arrival on his doorstep will change his life forever.

It's different for Annie McDermott. Gun or no gun, her life will stay pretty much the same. She will carry on doing the same job, come home every evening to the same welcoming smile, settle down in the same armchair. But she will never forget that she was a witness to this day's events. Annie is on her way to work. She doesn't know that before the next sunrise one of the people in this street will lie dead.

She crosses the road just in front of the green Rover and notices the two men sitting inside. There is something about their appearance that immediately puts her on edge, as if she has seen blood seeping from an old sack, or a dog cowering, drawing its tail just a little too tightly into its hind legs. The feeling is one of a spring being coiled, of horror just out of sight. The gaunt-looking man in his black leather bomber jacket catches her attention. Lean, hungry – that's how Annie sees him. A wolfman. She gives an involuntary shudder of unease, then immediately tells herself off for being a silly old goose.

The morning of Monday 5 December is drizzly and overcast. The whole town is fading to grey in the mist. And here are two men with nothing better to do than sit around in a car. Annie frowns and carries on to number nineteen, Rochester Avenue. It is a quarter past eleven and old Mrs Poole will be needing her shopping if she is to get the dinner on before her favourite show starts on daytime TV.

Moments later Father Thomas O'Leary pauses to look the car over. He too wonders what this odd couple of silent, unsmiling, middle-aged men are doing there. Father O'Leary has a feeling they're on surveillance of some kind. They might be police, he guesses, or maybe social security investigators. A couple of the houses in this road are privately rented – targets for benefit fraud perhaps. Still, there's no time for idle speculation. He is already late for his appointment.

Finally, postwoman Jenny Clarke is cycling back from her round when she almost collides with a schoolboy. He has stepped out in front of her without looking. Typical teenager! Not a thought in the world and not a care for anybody else. Plus, what's he doing out of school? As Jenny turns at the T-junction she looks back and glimpses two men getting out of the car and walking briskly towards the boy. Though she can't help wonder about it for a moment or two she soon puts it to the back of her mind. Little does she know that, within moments of that near-miss, the teenager will be running for his life.

Ian Moore belatedly tries to apologise to the postie, but she has already turned left and is pedalling towards the depot and a hot mug of tea. He sighs. Getting knocked on his backside by a stupid bike would just about round off a less than triumphant morning.

The reason he is back home at this time is because he was clowning around at school, trying to impress the girls in general and Vicky Shaw in particular. He was jumping down from a wall in the school grounds when he heard the seam rip. That's right – he's only split his pants, and right in front of the one girl in the whole of Year 9 he really fancies. Imagine if that postie really had knocked him over! Ian can just see himself lying flat on his back with his boxers showing through the split seam. Still, no harm done. A quick change and he will be back at school in time for French.

'So why am I in such an all-fired hurry?' he says out loud, his mind conjuring up the joys of *Les Magasins de Beauville*.

Could it be because Vicky is in the same set for French? That was the first lesson he plucked up courage to sit next to her. Guess what – she didn't even try to protest. He isn't mistaken. She really did keep edging gradually closer to him during the lesson, didn't she? She had to be aware that her bare forearm was touching his. It was an unforgettable moment for him. All the time her cool skin was touching his he was holding his breath, wanting the sensation to last forever. He smiles. The best-looking girl in the whole year and she likes him! Life is good. After all the years of moving from town to town he is settled. All those flats and rented houses and now he has somewhere he can call home. He is enjoying the luxury of having lived in the same house for three years. He has mates. He is doing well at school. Now it looks like he has a girlfriend too. Good? Life is *great*!

Swinging the front gate open, Ian walks up the garden path to the door. Still smiling at the thought of Vicky, he rummages in his pocket for his key. He comes across the crumpled authorisation slip from school, then a two-day-old newsletter he forgot to hand to Dad, before finally finding the front door key. That's when he notices the two men. They're heading his way. For some reason he can't fathom, the hairs on the back of his neck start to prickle. He senses danger just out of sight.

'Good morning,' says one of them.

Ian registers the thick Irish burr. The man sounds just like his dad.

'You must be Ian.'

Ian frowns. This is one of those primal fears they instil in you back in primary school: stranger danger. Ian might be a level-headed fourteen year old and not given to paranoia, but the alarm bells are already ringing. He doesn't recognise either the stocky, red-faced man approaching him or the taller, slightly balding man bringing up the rear. Instinctively Ian withdraws his key from the lock and squeezes it into his palm.

'Who wants to know?' he asks.

'Oh, this has to be Ian all right,' says the man closer to him. 'He's got his da's lip.' Ian doesn't like his tone of voice. It is cold, the way a fish on a slab is cold. Yes, that's just what Ian hears – a voice preserved in crushed ice. It is as if the man is being worked by a mechanism under the skin – clockwork menace.

'You know him then?' Ian asks, questions flashing through his mind. 'You know my dad?'

The Irish accents give him food for thought. They really do sound like the old man. Same intonation and everything.

'Oh, we know your da,' says the first, stocky man. 'Old acquaintances, that's us.' Shorty is leaning on the gates watching Ian and flicking the latch absent-mindedly. *Click, click, click* goes the cast iron fitting. The second man is standing just behind him, glancing occasionally up and down the road.

'So when would you be expecting your da home?'

Ian shrugs. He is usually an open, chatty lad, but not this time. You can be too friendly for your own good. The conversation reminds him of a scene from a bad gangster movie. He is half-expecting the men to ask him to go for a walk with them or make him an offer he can't refuse. Well, I rotten well will refuse, he thinks, you see if I don't.

'Will he be at work, do you think?'

Ian is feeling increasingly uneasy. Unease turns to anxiety when the questioner casually ups the ante:

'It's chilly out here,' he says. 'Maybe we could wait for him indoors.'

OK, that's one step too far. Ian slips the key back in his pocket and leaves his hand in there, covering it. Something is wrong here. Two complete strangers are asking to come inside the house and they are starting to get pushy about it.

'Who . . . who are you?' he asks, the words seeming to unravel as they leave his lips. 'Are you sure you know my dad?'

'Us? Oh, we're old friends of your daddy's, all right. We go way back.'

Ian listens to that gruff Irish burr. Close his eyes and he might almost think it was Dad. But for the first time in his life he finds the accent threatening. News footage flickers through his thoughts – of men in masks and sunglasses, of explosions, of figures in olive green fatigues firing volleys over a freshly-dug grave. A doubt takes root. Is Ian mistaken or did Dad watch those items with unusual intensity? Worrying associations are made in the back alleys of his mind.

'I don't know you,' he says.

The two men exchange glances.

'No,' says the shorter man, the one who is doing all the talking. 'You don't, but we know you. We were at your christening. Auld friends of the family, that's us.'

5

At my christening! Ian's eyes widen. Now he knows something is wrong. His early childhood is locked behind a series of doors, each one bolted and sealed against enquiry. The christening belongs to another life – a time his father skirts around, offering a minimum of information; a time that lies undisturbed behind the last of the locked and bolted doors, where hidden, unnamed demons dwell.

'Look,' Ian says, his voice reduced to a croak by the tightness in his throat. 'I can't let you in. I don't know either of you at all.'

His eyes sweep the street, looking for an escape route.

'If you want to see my dad you'd better call back.'

It is as if a thin cobweb of suspicion is being pulled over Ian's face. Next time the stocky man speaks the cobweb suddenly pulls skin tight.

'Now, we'd like to do that, Ian,' he says, 'we really would. But we're in a wee bit of a hurry, you see. So if you'll get that key out of your pocket and let us in we can all wait for Kenny boy together.'

Kenny. This time Ian's senses swim. He hasn't heard that name for years, not since he was a tiny boy bouncing on his daddy's knee, not since he was the apple of his daddy's eye, his poor dead mammy's too.

'I want you to go,' says Ian, struggling to control the tremble in his voice, trying to push the horror out of sight.

'Now, is that any way to talk to two of your da's oldest friends?' says the stocky man, his hand restlessly working the latch. *Click, click, click.*

The sleeve of his jacket slips back. Ian notices something – a patch of discoloured skin on his forearm. He is still staring when he sees the gun. The man's tight, greasy jacket is only fastened by one button and it gapes as he leans forward. The film of suspicion is transformed into a thin line of fright. It slices through Ian's flesh like cheesewire. The revolver is tucked into the man's waistband, pushed up against his paunch.

Ian is done talking now. He makes a break for it, vaulting over the wall between his house and the next door neighbour's. On his way over he raps his shin, but he keeps going. Barely keeping his balance, he half runs, half staggers to the road. By the time the two men react he has hit the pavement and is pounding towards the top of the road. As he skids round the corner he hears the stocky man's voice whipcrack through the air.

'Get after the wee–'

Then it's lost in the squeal of a lorry's airbrakes. For the second time that morning Ian Moore has stepped out into the road without looking. This time he has good cause, certainly better than a pair of torn pants or the memory of Vicky Shaw's cool skin. He is being chased by armed men. Now he isn't just a wee whatever-the-man-had-said, he is also a young idiot to boot. At least, that's according to the lorry driver.

From the window of Mrs Poole's living room, Annie McDermott sees it all, two grown men after a young boy. The fabric of normal life has just torn open. Menace has come spilling out. She phones the police.

'The things you read in the newspapers,' Annie says, by way of explanation, 'I can't just let this go.'

While Annie is telling the 999 operator what she has seen, Ian is racing down the main road towards the dual carriageway. His torn pants are forgotten. Fright is lodged in his throat like a plug of unswallowed food. He has somehow stepped out of his everyday world of torn pants and stolen looks at Vicky Shaw and into this other place where he knows neither the players nor the rules. He remembers movies in which fugitives run out into busy traffic, making horns blow and tyres squeal. Now he knows why they do it.

'Come back here!' shouts the taller of the two men, the wolfman. He has outpaced his shorter, more heavily-built partner and he is gaining on Ian.

'We only want to talk to you.'

You wanted to do a lot more than talk back there, Ian thinks. You wanted to invite yourself into my house. He concentrates on his stride. Keep it long, he tells himself. Don't let it shorten.

If I can just get among the traffic I've got a chance.

He sprints across two lanes and vaults over the railing on the central reservation. Terrified as he is, part of him, maybe only a tiny part, is exhilarated, living off every breathless, driving moment of the chase.

Ian is in luck. He arrives at the dual carriageway just as there is a break in the traffic. His pursuers aren't so fortunate. They are forced to stand, jumping about and peering between the speeding cars and lorries.

Ian makes for the subway under the flyover. Once through the subway he pounds up the escalator in the shopping centre, wincing at the way the metallic ring echoes through the shopping mall. At the top he scans the flyover and the roadway for signs of the men. He is in the clear. He almost vomits. His heartbeat slowly begins to return to normal. He forces the sour taste out of his mouth. Instinct starts to loosen its grip and the thinking part of him takes over.

'I've got to phone Dad,' he pants.

Punching in the number of Dad's mobile, he holds the set to his head.

Kenny. They called him Kenny.

It's engaged. Shoving the phone irritably in his pocket, Ian looks around, half-expecting to see the men walking

8

towards him. There is no sign of them. The midday shoppers are thin on the ground so it won't be difficult to spot them. Then the thought strikes him. They've got a car. You idiot! He wants to yell. You saw them getting out of it.

What make of car was it? Think!

It's big, maybe a two-litre job – he remembers that much – and it's green. What do they call that colour? Yes, racing green, that's it. Ian watches the traffic on the dual carriageway and on the flyover. Nothing. No, he's wrong. There, pulling up at the entrance to the high-rise car park, is a racing green saloon. Ian sees the wolfman getting out and shrinks back. His heart kicks in his chest. The plug of vomit rises. 'They're coming!'

What do these men want with his dad? Is his old fella in some kind of trouble? All the old doubts resurface. Why were they always on the move? Why was there no family to speak of? Why did they never put down roots? Ian runs the film of his childhood through his mind and he knows he can't go running to the police.

'Jeez, Dad, what have you got yourself into here?'

Ian's mind is racing to find a way out of the shopping centre. He settles on Trafalgar Way and starts to jog in that direction. By now the wolfman will be making his way into the main concourse. The stocky one will be parking the car and heading for the stairs. Ian can hear his own breathing, snatched and irregular.

'It's now or never.'

He reaches the top of the escalator and his legs turn to water. There at the bottom stands the wolfman. Hard eyes fix him. He spins on his heel and sprints in the opposite direction. His heart is banging, a heat rash sweeping up his back and over his neck.

This can't be happening!

An hour ago it was an ordinary school day. All he had to

think about was French and Vicky and pizza from the school canteen. Now he's a hunted animal.

He is at the corner of Nelson Walk when he looks back. The wolfman is stepping off the escalator. He doesn't run. He is content to keep Ian in sight. He's walking towards the boy, quickly enough to stay in touch but not quickly enough to draw attention to himself.

Soon Ian will be trapped. His eyes drift from the wolfman and cast about, desperate to find an escape route. Then he hears a loud clang behind him. A delivery man has just wheeled a trolley out of a service lift and is pushing it into the rear entrance of one of the shops. He is in mid-delivery and there are two more loads still to move. There is a concertina gate and the delivery man has left it open. It is all the invitation Ian needs. He almost flies to the lift.

'Wait!'

The wolfman loses his composure and makes a grab for Ian. In response, Ian wrenches back the concertina gate. To his horror, it sticks. He tugs again. Still jammed.

'You're coming with me,' the wolfman says, reaching through after Ian, while Ian bats at the invading hand. 'Don't be stupid, son. It's just a word we want.'

With a defiant jut of his jaw Ian gives one last, desperate yank at the concertina gates. Wolfie snatches his hand back just in time to avoid it being trapped.

'Ow!'

A charge like electricity runs the length of Ian's arm. In his hurry to get the lift door shut, he has pinched his right hand in the concertina mechanism and gouged a lump out of the fleshy part of his palm. Drops of dark blood are falling on the floor. Sickened by the pain but still determined to get away, he thumps the Down button and leaves the wolfman behind.

Looking around, Ian's eyes light on the pallets. They're

loaded with jeans. He checks the labels. It's the new DNA label everybody's gone crazy about. Decent enough jeans but what's with all the dangly bits? They have this silver double helix hanging from the belt. DNA – get it? Plus, they trade on this scally image, with a steel comb attached to the back pocket. The TV ad has caused a big fuss about glamorising yob culture with the line: 'Wear DNAs with your DMs.' Ian shakes his head: naffissimo. The top pair is a couple of sizes too big but he doesn't have time to go through them.

'Close enough,' he decides. 'It isn't as if I've got much choice. They'll have to do.' He doesn't like taking them but beggars can't be choosers. I'm being chased by armed men, he thinks. Normal rules no longer apply.

Binding his right hand with his handkerchief, Ian throws his torn trousers into a corner of the lift and tucks his tie and blazer in a hastily rolled-up bundle under his arm. He is wriggling into the jeans when something sticks into the small of his back – the steel comb has a particularly sharp handle.

'What a stupid thing to carry,' he says. 'You could do yourself a mischief.'

The lift stops and Ian finds himself in a basement loading bay that smells of oil and petrol. Fortunately for him, it's deserted. There are only the distant echoes of men's voices to tell him he isn't completely alone. Whether there are witnesses to his passage through the loading bay or not, Ian is able to walk unchallenged up the ramp to street level. Darting glances out until he is satisfied that he isn't being followed, he joins the office workers who are now thronging the sandwich bars. His watch tells him it is midday.

He finds a discarded plastic bag in an ornamental flower bed and uses it to carry his uniform. That done, he makes his way to the bus stops. He takes the first bus that comes.

The destination doesn't matter just so long as he is able to put some distance between himself and the men – the two armed men.

Two

There isn't a moment of the journey when Ian isn't flashing looks out of the window, imagining a racing green saloon car pulling alongside. A gun – a *gun* for crying out loud! How could this happen? In the whirling snowstorm of his thoughts, Ian has awarded the two men superpowers. *You can run*, he imagines them saying in classic hard man fashion, *but you can't hide*.

No, that's ridiculous. I have run and I'm hiding right now. They're not so great. In the shopping centre I outpaced and outwitted the pair of them. Ian smiles as he remembers the clang of the concertina door. He remembers the look on the wolfman's face as he snatches back his hand and pounds impotently while the lift descends. *You're not so superior.*

Come to think of it, the short, fat guy is so slow he would be comic – but for the gun, of course. It all comes down to that, doesn't it? The gun.

'Excuse me,' Ian asks the old lady in front, 'isn't the park up here somewhere?'

'The park?' she repeats. 'Yes, it's the next stop but one.'

'Thanks.'

Ian rubs the condensation from the window and looks

outside. The winter sun has broken through the banks of grey cloud and its watery light is gleaming on the wet road surface, transforming it into a mirror. He consults his watch. He has already missed French . . . and Vicky Shaw.

'This is the park coming up now,' the old lady tells him.

'Cheers,' says Ian, glad of some friendly human contact.

Once off the bus, he jogs into the park and sits down on the first bench. It is dedicated to Albert and Marjorie Halliday, whoever they are. Ian checks his hand. The bleeding has almost stopped. Wrapping the bloodstained handkerchief back round the wound, he pulls out his mobile and calls Dad.

'Come on, come on!' he murmurs.

What if Dad goes home? It's possible. He's self-employed, a mobile tradesman. He doesn't have an office or a depot to return to so home will be his first destination if he finishes his jobs. What if he walks straight into Little and Large? Just when Ian is about to give up, Dad answers.

'Dad, where are you?'

In the van. That's good.

'Listen, whatever you do, don't go home. There were these two men at the house. What? No, I had to go home early. I split my pants.'

Oh, this is great! Dad has started quizzing him about his stupid trousers, of all things.

'Look,' says Ian, 'shut up about the pants, will you? You're not listening to me. There were two men at the house. What? Yes, two of them, heavy-looking characters.'

He's finally got Dad's attention.

'They gave me the creeps, Dad, they really did. They wanted me to let them in the house. No, of course I didn't. The point is they were getting really pushy so I did a runner on them. I couldn't think of anything else to do.'

He pauses, wishing there was another way of putting this.

'One of them had a gun.'

Ian has imagined all sorts of reactions but not this one. Dad is silent at the other end of the phone. No exclamation, no questions, no disbelief – he is just breathing low and tense into the phone. Ian starts wondering if he is still there.

'Did you hear what I said?'

Still no answer.

'Dad?'

'I'm here.'

'Then speak to me. Do you know what all this is in aid of?'

Dad answers with a simple, 'I know.'

'It isn't the police, is it?'

'No.'

'But you do know what it's about?'

'Yes.'

Ian wants to scream down the phone.

What's with the monosyllables? Speak to me. I'm your son.

'Then don't you think you should let me in on it? They scared me witless back there. I mean, are you in trouble or something?'

'I'm not discussing this over the phone, Ian. I'll come to meet you. Where are you?'

'Queen's Park. Tell you what, I'll meet you at the bandstand.'

'I'll be there in ten minutes,' says Dad. 'Just sit tight.'

'But what's it all about?'

'Ten minutes, Ian. Ten minutes.'

Back in Rochester Avenue, Annie McDermott opens the

door to the police. She is agitated. Nothing like this has ever happened to her before. She's fifty-two years old. She's a home help. Once a week she goes line dancing with her husband. Twice a week she goes to the bingo with her sister. She is happy to potter along. It isn't often the ugly side of life comes calling. Her idea of a crisis is the drains backing up or the Lottery machine at the newsagents going on the blink.

'Well?' she asks.

'We couldn't find anything,' says the first officer. 'There was no sign of the two men, or of the teenage boy. Can you put a name to any of them?'

Annie's brow furrows.

'I didn't recognise those men,' she says. 'They looked . . .' She searches for the word. 'They looked *shady*.'

She shouts in to Mrs Poole.

'What's the name of that young lad at number sixteen?' she asks.

'The Moore boy?' says Mrs Poole. 'Ian.'

'Ian Moore,' says the officer, making a note of the name. 'So he's the one they were chasing?'

Annie nods.

'Ian's a nice boy,' says Mrs Poole, walking in from the kitchen. 'Not like some of the youths that hang around here.'

The policeman sighs, anticipating a lecture on law and order and the lack of bobbies on the beat. It doesn't come. Instead Mrs Poole adds an extra bit of information.

'The father's name is Peter.'

'There's no Mrs Moore then?'

'No,' says Mrs Poole, giving the matter some thought. 'Peter's a widower. I'm sure he told me that once. Don't take it for gospel, but I'm pretty sure he's a widower. He's very quiet, you see – so is his son. They keep themselves to themselves.'

'You're quite sure what you saw, Mrs McDermott?' the first officer asks. 'These men were definitely chasing Ian?'

'You should have seen them,' Annie tells him, slightly nettled that he is questioning her judgement. 'They were up to no good. I'm not making this up.'

'No, I'm sure you're not, but people can be mistaken. You'd be surprised–'

'I am *not* mistaken,' says Annie fiercely. 'That poor lad looked terrified, as if he was running for his life.'

'We'll take one more look round,' the officer tells her, 'then we'll put in a report.'

'That's it?' Annie says, horrified. 'A *report*? What if that youngster really is in trouble?'

'We're not ignoring it, Mrs McDermott,' the officer insists. 'We are going to look into it.'

Annie shows the officers out. She isn't happy.

Nor is Ian. By now it is nearly twenty to one. Dad is over five minutes late. You'd think he could be on time for *this*.

'Come on, come *on*!'

Ian is feeling very exposed hanging round the bandstand like this, as if the two men might appear at any moment. He watches a grey squirrel scamper across the path and looks at his watch for the hundredth time.

'Come on, Dad. What's keeping you?'

Ian remembers what the stocky man called Dad. 'Kenny.'

He mulls the name over. The ghost of a memory hovers in the far depths of his memory, then is gone. Finally Dad arrives. He looks Ian up and down, his gaze settling on the jeans that hang in folds over his shoes.

'Where did you get those jeans?'

'I took them.'

'What do you mean, took them?'

'OK, if you really want to know, I stole them.'

'You did what!'

'Dad, in my place you would have done exactly the same. I had no choice.'

'We all have choices,' Dad says abruptly.

He seems to be trying to make a point but it is lost on Ian.

'Start at the beginning,' Dad says, finally putting the matter of the stolen clothes to one side. 'Tell me everything. Everything, you understand? This is important, Ian. Don't leave out a thing.'

Ian nods. They set off towards the lake, walking slowly. From time to time Dad stops dead and asks Ian to repeat something. He seems obsessed by Ian's descriptions of the two men, especially the stocky one. He goes over them three times before he is satisfied.

'Two men,' he says over and over. 'You're sure there were two?'

'Positive.'

'Did you notice anything about them? Any identifying marks?'

Ian thinks.

'Yes, the fat one had something wrong with his arm. A patch of skin was a different colour.'

Dad flinches visibly. The fact is significant.

'They didn't see you get on the bus, did they?' he asks. 'You're absolutely certain that they didn't see you?'

His eyes were pleading. That's the thing that really has Ian rattled – the fear in his father's eyes. It isn't long ago he used to think the old man was a giant – good at most things, afraid of absolutely nothing. At this moment he is as vulnerable as a small child, as fragile as cut glass.

'I said so, didn't I?'

In truth, Ian isn't certain of anything any more. The whole morning is like some bizarre fantasy. He is finding it hard to believe it himself.

'That's all right, son. I believe you.'

Dad turns to face Ian.

'Listen. We've got to go.'

Ian's heart tears as surely as if a shard of glass has ripped clean through it. He's heard those words too often before to miss their meaning.

'Go?'

'Yes, right away.'

'You mean leave town, don't you?'

Dad nods.

'I'm afraid so. I know you've made friends, son. I thought this was the last move. I honestly did. I even bought the house, I was that sure.'

Ian's face is a picture of misery.

'Look, you have to believe me, son. I wish there was some alternative, but there isn't.'

Ian throws back his head.

'Oh, why now?'

'Ian, I wouldn't do this if it wasn't necessary. You understand that, don't you?'

'That's just it,' Ian says wearily, thinking of all the other moves. 'I don't understand at all. Why won't you tell me what all this is about?'

'I can't,' says Dad, squinting against the sunlight.

The morning mist and drizzle have faded.

Ian stiffens.

'Can't?' he says. 'Or won't? Surely you can go to the police?'

'I wish it was that simple,' says Dad.

'Well, I'm not doing anything,' says Ian. 'Not unless I

get an explanation. I'm fourteen, Dad, not a kid any more. You can't make me.'

Dad seizes him by the arms and stares into his eyes with a kind of desperate rage.

'Can't make you, eh? Want to take a bet on that?'

His breath is hot on Ian's face. The grip of his fingers is hard enough to make Ian wince.

'You don't get it, do you?' Dad says, even more fiercely, more wound up, if anything. 'These men don't play games.'

'Don't you think I know that?' Ian cries, pulling free. 'I'm the one who saw the gun, remember?'

He waits a beat before adding: 'Dad, they're criminals, aren't they? Are you in some kind of trouble?'

Dad raises his face to the sky and groans.

'Son, you don't know the half of it.'

'Then tell me. Whatever it is, I can take it. If these men are after you then I'm in danger too. Dad, you can't wrap me in cotton wool any more. Whatever you've got yourself into, it's had me bouncing round the country until I don't know where I am. You owe me.'

Dad stands by the edge of the lake looking out across the water. It is some time before he speaks.

'The men who came to the door,' he says finally, 'I owe them money.'

'How much?'

Dad lowers his eyes for a moment then, once again, he looks straight at Ian.

'Two hundred thousand pounds.'

Dad's reply hits Ian like a sledgehammer. It snatches the breath right out of his chest. The most money he has seen in one go is the handful of tenners you take from an automated cash machine.

'How much?' he gasps.

This time Dad delivers the words in a slow, even monotone. For a moment Ian thinks he can actually hear a note of pride in Dad's voice. He repeats it.

'I owe them two . . . hundred . . . thousand . . . pounds.'

For the last few seconds Ian has been treading the waters of his new reality. He goes under then splutters to the surface.

'But how could you? I mean, I've never even seen that kind of money in my life. If you've got that sort of money stashed away, how come I never see any of it?'

Dad's face wears a grim smile.

'Because I've still got the money intact – well, some of it.'

Ian shakes his head.

'I don't get it. If you've got two hundred grand, why not use it?'

'I bought the house. I didn't want to spend the rest.'

'Why not?'

'Lots of reasons.'

Ian is losing patience.

'Such as?' he says.

'I was scared to spend it all. I always had this feeling they were on my tail, that I might have to do a runner. I've been keeping it for emergencies.'

'So this *is* an emergency?' Ian asks.

'Oh yes. They don't come much bigger.'

'And all the other times we moved, they were emergencies too?'

Dad nods.

'Oh come on, Dad – give. Who are these men?'

'From the description you've given me,' Dad replies, 'the tall fellow is Billy McClean. The boss man goes by the name of Chubby Barr.'

'Chubby?'

The nickname suits the stocky man down to the ground.

'His real name is Jimmy Barr, but everybody calls him Chubby.'

'Who are they?' Ian asks. 'Gangsters?'

The question doesn't connect. Dad slips away from it.

'Come on, son,' says Dad, cutting the conversation dead. 'We're wasting time. We can talk on the way to the car.'

They start climbing the steepest slope in the park, where it curves past a broad, flat acacia tree. A grey squirrel scampers across the grass then pauses to look at them, as if he too is trying to work out Dad's secret.

'Chubby and Billy didn't start out as gangsters,' says Dad. 'None of us did.'

Ian frowns. He is still waiting for something to make sense.

'The Troubles made us,' Dad says. 'That's where it all began.'

'The Troubles?' Ian repeats. 'You mean this started back in Ireland?'

Dad nods.

'Belfast. Aye.'

'Are you IRA or something?'

Dad chuckles.

'Wrong side, son. Wrong side.'

He presses the alarm fob. The van headlights flash a couple of times and the alarm gives a brief yelp.

'So where did this money come from?' Ian asks.

'Not out here,' says Dad, even though there is nobody within a hundred yards. 'Let's get in the van.'

Dad takes the radio fascia out of the glove compartment. As he clicks it in place the inside of the van is flooded with sound. The DJ is running through the headlines that will be in the news *at the top of the hour*. With a frown, Dad lowers the volume.

'I did a bank job,' he says, reversing the vehicle.

'You did what!'

Ian stares at his father as if he is seeing him for the first time. Dad – the single parent, ever-present in his life. Dour, dependable, law-abiding Dad, the man who tuts disapprovingly at items on the early evening news, a *bank robber*!

'But you can't have!'

It doesn't make sense. When did you have the opportunity? All through primary school there was hardly a day you didn't pick me up from school or from a child-minder and spent the rest of the evening with me.

When? Ian thinks. When?

In all the years they have been a family of two they can't have been apart more than a couple of days. There is no wider family to speak of and they have few close friends. Ian has wondered about that from time to time, compared his situation with the family lives of his classmates. He has quizzed Dad, begged for details, but always been fobbed off. Ian's mind is racing. When could Dad have done it? There was one time. He was twelve. Dad allowed him to go away for the weekend with Gareth Evans's family to their caravan in Pwhelli. Ian wondered about it at the time. Why would Dad, usually so protective, suddenly let him go all the way to north Wales?

Was that it? Is that when you did it?

Ian's curiosity gets the better of him.

'When did this happen?' he blurts.

Dad cranes his neck to check the traffic before turning right on to Park Avenue.

'It was when you were a tiny wee boy, barely walking.'

The leafless tress flash by. Not the Wales weekend then.

'Back in Belfast.'

Ian isn't making any sense of this.

'But that must have been over ten years ago.'

'Eleven.'

'I don't get it. That's ancient history. So how could it come back to haunt us now?'

Dad pulls up at lights and shifts in his seat. Looking straight at Ian he says: 'We grew up in a war zone, Chubby, Billy and I. Men have long memories there.'

That just doesn't wash. There's got to be so much more to this. The unanswered question hangs like a cloud.

'But eleven years!'

The driver behind sounds his horn. The lights have changed to green. Dad holds up his hand in acknowledgement and pulls away.

'More than eleven, son,' he says. 'More than eleven.'

Three

There were four of them in the car. REM was playing on the radio. Billy McClean was at the wheel, drumming his fingers to 'Sidewinder'. James 'Chubby' Barr sat beside him in the passenger seat. He was wearing a satisfied grin and he turned round regularly to share the events of the raid with the men in the back, Hugh McCullough and Kenny Kincaid. McCullough laughed and joked with Barr. Kenny was a different matter. He sat, his face lost in shadow. He was pretending to sleep. There was a purpose to his dozing: to declare himself, if only in his own mind, separate, a man apart.

'Did you see the look on that counter clerk's face, Kenny boy?' Barr chuckled. 'Like John Hurt when the alien poked through his belly.'

Kenny didn't answer. He was determined to keep up the pretence of sleep, but in his mind's eye he was re-living the whole thing. He felt the woollen balaclava on his face, saw its loose threads flickering before his eyes. Under the bright striplights of the bank he saw terrified customers flattening themselves on the floor, trying to claw their way into it as if it would save them should it come to shooting.

Mostly, he felt the shotgun in his hand.

Its weight.

Its coldness.

Its danger.

And all the while, through the whole episode, in some unknown way, he knew that something had changed. He'd had enough.

'I thought the wee mammy's boy was going to pee his pants,' McCullough roared.

The others joined in but Kenny kept his own counsel. He could still hear the screams when Hugh McCullough drove the stock of his shotgun into the manager's stomach.

With his eyes closed and his head lying to one side rocking while the car bumped down the country lane, Kenny wondered what he was doing here. The same thought had been throbbing away in his brain for weeks: I can't do this any more.

'Will you look at him?' Barr said. 'We drive away with getting on for a quarter of a million quid and there's Kenny Kincaid sleeping like a baby.'

Barr nodded approvingly. This was the kind of thing that earned his respect – a man who could walk into a bank in broad daylight carrying a shotgun then act as if nothing had happened.

'Cool as a cucumber, that's Kenny.'

'He doesn't give much away, does he?' said McCullough.

Hugh McCullough was one of those men who start to go bald in their twenties. What with his deep, sunken eyes, chiselled cheekbones and square jaw, his head was beginning to resemble the skull underneath his skin.

'No,' Chubby replied. 'Poker-face, that's what we called Kenny at school. There was this one time we all copied his homework. Remember that, do you, Billy?'

Billy McClean grunted, concentrating on his driving. It was misty and he wasn't sure of the road back from Portadown.

'A whole double lesson we had to stand out at the front of the class. Our English teacher Mr Campbell wanted to know who had copied and who had let his work be copied, as if it made much difference. He must have known, of course. Kenny's the only one out of the lot of us with even half a brain. But did we crack? Not a single person. And when it came to the cane, do you know what Kenny did? Mr Campbell, who fancied himself as a tough guy and a man who could hand out the discipline, finished giving us his six strokes and we all put our hands away under our armpits where they started throbbing like crazy. Not Kenny – he just held his hand out. Not a shake, not a quiver. I tell you, he's an iceman.'

In the back of the car, in the dark, Kenny stirred.

Iceman. I'm an iceman.

'Then,' Barr continued, 'he looked Mr Campbell in the eye, cool as you like, as if he was asking for half a dozen more. A hard man in the making, that was young Kenny Kincaid.'

He leaned over the seat rest, waving a fat palm in front of Kenny's face.

'Are you awake there, Kenny boy?' he asked. 'We're talking about you.'

Kenny was awake, but he wasn't about to answer. By pretending to sleep he had put himself in a place where they couldn't reach him, a place where he didn't have to do this any more. He had a place like that when he was a wee boy – a den he made down by the railway tracks. Now that he was a man he had rebuilt the den in his head, constructed a private refuge where the world could not come.

Kenny remembered Mr Campbell's six strokes as if it were yesterday. He remembered how his hand hurt. Mr Campbell had been disappointed in him, so disappointed Kenny had had to force himself to look the teacher in the *eye. He was Mr Campbell's star pupil, but here he was behaving like the worst kind of young tough, throwing his future away, so Mr Campbell poured all that frustration into the strokes he gave young Master Kenneth Kincaid. Didn't he beat the foolish young whelp with twice the force he had shown any of the others? Didn't he score his palms with thick, red welts of pain?*

But most of all Kenny remembered the way he had to prove himself a man by holding out his hand for more, even though it was aching right down to the marrow of his bones.

A man! That's a laugh.

Thirteen he was when Campbell laid the stick across his palm and even then he was set on a road that would lead to blood, sacrifice and exile.

'Anyway,' Barr said, jerking Kenny back into the present, 'it's time we calmed down a wee bit. We don't want to go drawing attention to ourselves, do we? Not when we've got two hundred grand plus small change in used notes in the boot.'

Barr looked at tight-lipped, frozen-faced Billy McClean hunched over the wheel and couldn't resist one last bit of banter.

'Hey Billy,' Barr said, nudging the taciturn driver, 'didn't you hear what we said? Don't be getting yourself excited there. Calm down, Billy boy.'

Skull-headed McCullough roared appreciatively from the back then the car went quiet, only the final bars of 'Sidewinder' breaking the silence. In the distance they could see the gantries of the Harland and Wolff shipyard, like crouching giants. They would be in Belfast in twenty minutes.

Four

Dad takes a left and drives down an unapproved road that runs along the railway viaduct. They pass the stone pile of the central library on the corner. Ian remembers he's got a couple of books overdue. One is *The Thirty-Nine Steps*.

'Where are we going?' he asks as they enter the odd, self-contained world that exists in the shadow of the viaduct.

'I've got a lock-up down here.'

'Is that where you keep it?' Ian asks. 'The money, I mean.'

Dad doesn't answer. He doesn't need to. He parks the van by a unit set into the railway arches. Without a word, he walks over to a set of doors with peeling olive-green paintwork. The colour reminds Ian of military fatigues. A bit of a coincidence really, given what Dad has just told him.

'What are we doing here?' Ian asks, winding down his window.

Dad swings the door open. Inside there is a blue Volkswagen. Dad slides between the car and the wall and starts rummaging in the shadows at the back of the lock-up. Ian hears something scraping. Loose bricks are being removed from the wall. Dad emerges with a plain blue sports bag. Ian gets out of the car and walks over.

'Is this it?' he asks, looking down at the holdall. It's covered with brick dust and mortar.

Dad nods.

'That's it.'

Ian's heart slams in his chest.

'Can I see?'

Dad picks up the holdall and hoists it on the VW's bonnet. He opens it then unzips a large plastic folder inside. Finally he steps back. Ian looks at the contents.

'What's this stuff?'

He expects to see notes. But this is a collection of bank books, certificates, documents.

'You didn't think I'd still have the money, did you?' Dad says. 'I've salted it away in a series of accounts. Some of it is in bonds.'

Ian looks at the bewildering array of documentation.

'How did you know what to do?'

Dad shrugs.

'Doing what I did,' he says, 'you develop certain skills.'

Ian's eyes ask him to explain.

'You may have heard of money laundering.'

Maybe there isn't any money to see but Ian's throat goes dry, not with excitement but with fear – cold, naked fear. This much money could cause of lot of trouble. He senses a pact with the Devil. He can almost smell the brimstone.

'Is that how much there is, Dad, £200,000?'

'Some of it's gone,' Dad tells him, deadpan. 'I spent about £10,000 giving us a start over here. I bought the house three years ago for £75,000. I've used maybe another £20,000.'

'So over £100,000 of it has already gone!' Ian gasps. 'You've spent half?'

Dad closes the holdall.

'It took me eight years to decide to buy the house. I thought we were finally safe, you see.'

Ian stares at the holdall, unable to believe the turn his life has taken. The news is just finishing.

'So what's the VW in aid of?' Ian asks.

It is obviously part of the other £20,000.

Dad doesn't answer. Instead he slides into the driver's seat and reverses out. Still without a word he drives the van they came in into the lock-up in place of the VW.

Ian has the answer to his question.

'You mean we're going now!'

Dad doesn't answer. He pulls a few carrier bags off hooks on the wall. Ian reads the store names. They're all designer labels. They're obviously for him, replacements for the wardrobe full of gear back home that Dad is expecting him to abandon. Normally Ian would be excited by the purchases, but the new clothes mean another rented house in another town. It means walking away from a school where he is doing well. It means forgetting about Vicky.

'These are for you,' says Dad, throwing the stuff into the boot of the VW. 'They'll keep you going until we're settled and I can buy you more.'

He takes the carrier bag containing Ian's uniform and tosses it into the lock-up. It is his way of saying: *You won't be needing this.*

'These are my size,' says Ian.

'So?'

'But I thought these men coming was a surprise. You said you didn't know anything about it.'

'I didn't. Every few months I buy new stuff, just in case. There was a good chance they'd come sometime. Bit like a boy scout, I suppose – I'm always prepared.'

'You had all this planned!' Ian cries.

'Grow up,' says Dad. 'I *always* have this planned. Even when I thought we were off the hook I spent a few hours a week bringing everything up to date. What do you expect – that I'm going to take chances with our lives? Every time I've suspected they were getting close, I've had to do this. Sometimes we've had to clear out at a minute's notice. So there's an escape kit always ready – money, change of ID, a couple of sets of clothes, a car.'

That's when Ian remembers.

'The nativity!' he cries. 'I was six and I was going to be Joseph in the Christmas play. It was the night of the performance. You just threw me in the back of the car and drove us out of town.'

He looks into the distance.

'I was so scared and ashamed. I knew I was letting everybody down. That's right, I remember it now. I was bawling my eyes out. That was all because of the money, wasn't it?'

Dad finishes throwing bags and boxes into the boot of the car.

'It was because of the police.'

'The police? You mean they tried to arrest you?'

Dad shakes his head.

'Not that kind of police. I'm talking about Special Branch – the ones that deal with politics, the hard stuff. They came looking for me too. They wanted me to turn supergrass. They had Chubby and the boys banged up but they wouldn't talk. The peelers wanted me to spill my guts about the leadership of the organisation.'

'So you ran?'

'Yes, I ran. My card's marked. Nobody likes a tout.'

Tout. The word is unfamiliar but Ian knows exactly what it means.

'That's the whole point,' Ian retorts bitterly. 'How am I supposed to know? I haven't got a clue.'

He wants to pinch himself just to make sure he is having this conversation.

'Put yourself in my shoes, Dad. What do I actually know about you?'

He waves away his father's attempt at a protest, then continues.

'You, my own dad – all of a sudden it's like you're a complete stranger. I know you came over here from Ireland sometime. Pretty obvious really, I suppose, what with the accent and all.'

He laughs out loud.

'I didn't even know if you were a Catholic or a Protestant.'

'You didn't ask,' Dad says by way of reply. 'So I didn't burden you with it.'

'And what would you have told me if I did ask?' Ian demands. 'It's not like you ever gave much away. I've grown up without a mum, without grandparents, without a family.'

'Except me,' Dad reminds him.

'Yes,' Ian says. 'Except you, and now I find out that you're . . .'

He shakes his head and leans back against the VW. His hands flop in bewilderment by his side.

'Dad, you're a stranger.'

It takes Dad a few moments to react.

'No,' he says after a few moments. 'Don't you ever say that. Look at me, Ian. I'm the same man who's brought you up all these years. Son, I know this is hard but you must try to understand.'

'How?' Ian protests. 'Go on, tell me how. So far all I know is that you were one of these – these paramilitaries

33

and you robbed a bank. Then you did a runner. Tell me if I've missed something.'

At the police station the CID are looking over what they've got. It doesn't amount to much: two men chasing a boy, the theft of a pair of jeans, and an abandoned pair of trousers in a lift belonging to the same boy – Ian Moore. The police have identified the trousers' owner by the authorisation of absence slip they found in the pocket. Finally there is the detail that made them look closer at the sequence of events; bloodstains on the lift floor and on the trousers. Detective Sergeant Mark Lomas reviews the items and the notes made by the two PCs earlier in the day.

'What on earth is going on?' he murmurs.

Nobody in the room has got even the beginnings of an answer.

Five

It was dusk when Kenny Kincaid visited his wife's grave. These last minutes spent by her tiny but well-maintained plot proved to be the longest goodbye of his life. From where he stood with his sleeping young son, Kenny could see Harland and Wolff and the glowering ridge of the Cave Hill. The city's dark, ponderous landmarks were retreating slowly into the hazy twilight, blurring, becoming indistinct. They were giants slipping into dreamtime. How Kenny wanted the old loyalties to do the same, to soften and fade until nobody knew where a Prod ended and a Catholic began. He'd had it with all that.

The hatred had cost him too much: the end of his childhood, friendships, a wife.

Kenny stood looking at Tina's stone and at the napping child in the buggy. He tidied the plot one last time then stood bolt upright in a silent salute to a life that had given him so much joy, but whose end had split his heart in two. After a few moments he gripped the buggy's handles until his knuckles whitened round them. The pain of the present and fear for the future coiled round his heart. Then somebody broke in on his thoughts.

'I thought I'd find you here, Kenny,' said the speaker.

Kenny stiffened. He recognised the voice immediately.

'Good evening to you, Mr Hagan,' he said without so much as turning his head.

'Hello there.'

DCI Hagan was a grey-haired, thickset man. He couldn't have been any craggier if he'd been hewn out of the surrounding hills. He stood alongside Kenny, squinting through the murk.

'You miss her badly, don't you, son?'

Kenny listened with a closed expression. Son? Hagan was only five years his senior.

'You're not here to give me your condolences, Mr Hagan,' Kenny answered, 'so let's cut to the chase. You want something. What is it?'

Hagan smiled awkwardly. Nobody ever felt at ease with the policeman. It was as if the two sides of his face didn't quite match. That's what had earned him his nickname, Two Face. Some put it down to his time as a promising amateur boxer – in Belfast there was no shortage of fists ready to rearrange your face. Others said it was the legacy of a car bombing – an assassination attempt he had been lucky to survive. Most of Kenny's acquaintances put it more sourly. All peelers turn out like that, they said – two-faced.

'Why, have we got an arrangement?' he asked.

'No,' said Kenny. 'That's the point. There's no use following me around, Mr Hagan. I won't be any man's tout.'

'You're loyal, Kenny,' said Hagan. 'I'll give you that.'

He blew his nose and concluded with words as crisp as the evening chill.

'Pity the men you're loyal to aren't worth the dirt on your shoe.'

Kenny Kincaid wasn't a man to fall for flattery.

'I'm no different to any other man round here,' he said,

still looking straight ahead. 'I've done what was asked of me, no more, no less.'

Hagan dug his hands in his coat pockets. He didn't bother enquiring what had been asked of Kenny Kincaid. He had a good idea already.

'You're not afraid to be seen talking to a peeler then?' he said.

'Afraid?' Kenny repeated. 'No. I've told the boys the police have been hanging round me. They're not surprised. I'm not the only one you've approached, am I?'

Hagan gave his lop-sided grin.

'I wouldn't be doing my job if you were.'

He squeezed Kenny's arm.

'I'll be seeing you around, Kenny.'

Kenny didn't reply. He laid his flowers on Tina's grave and checked that baby Ian was warm enough. By the time he looked up the policeman had reached the cemetery gates. There the big man appeared to pause before turning slowly and retracing his steps.

'There is one thing,' Hagan said from a couple of metres away.

'And what's that, Mr Hagan?'

'Have you heard about the Portadown bank raid?'

There was no point denying it. Everybody had heard about it.

'I have.'

'But you don't know anything about it, do you?'

'No, Mr Hagan, I don't.'

Kenny delivered his reply in a controlled, even voice, the one he had practised back at the Academy with Mr Campbell, when he was learning to be a hard man. Hagan replied in his usual flat, slightly disappointed monotone. Success didn't come often in his job, but he was a patient man.

'Of course you don't, Kenny. Of course you don't.'

With that, Hagan took his leave for the second time. On this occasion he continued through the gates to his car. Kenny heard the engine cough into life. The conversation with Hagan had only confirmed that he had made the right decision. Whatever the risks in running, staying would be worse. The money from the bank raid was his passport out of here.

When he switched off the lights at half past eleven the next night it was in a hotel bedroom in the centre of Manchester. He sat listening to Ian's steady breathing then crossed to the plastic tray with its coffee-making set. By the flickering light of the TV set he poured the plastic carton of UHT milk into his decaf and sipped it. The coffee was hot but it did nothing to warm him. All the coals of Hell couldn't have managed that.

Kenny stood in the room, coffee cup in hand. He had turned the TV's volume down to zero and was watching the images flash across the screen as he channel-surfed. He wasn't looking for anything in particular – he just wanted something to take his mind off the money.

One part of him looked at the bundle of banknotes and saw a big house, a new car, the odd holiday abroad, a new start for his son – everything he'd always wanted. Another part of him looked and saw Kenny Kincaid as a marked man, a fugitive staring down the barrel of a gun.

What he had just done fairly made his head spin. It had been many months in the making. Ever since Tina's death he had been looking for a way out. All the time he had been acting like a loyal member of the organisation, he had been laying his plans. Finally, with the bank raid under his belt and knowing that Chubby, Billy and Hugh had gone to Lurgan 'on business', he had made his move. On a busy drinking night he had walked into Sam Mitchell's bar and casually taken the money from the safe. Knowing the share-out was the next day, Sam had asked him what he was doing. Though his blood was roaring in his head, Kenny's answer had sounded cool: 'Something's going on. That's why they've gone over to Lurgan. Give Chubby a ring if you want. He told me to move it.'

If he was believed he was on his way to England, if not he would be found in a day or two with his brains blown out. In the event, Sam shrugged and went back behind the bar. All those years Kenny and Chubby had been insepar-able counted for something. Kenny felt the weight of the bag. It would be like winning the pools, he told himself.

Without once looking to right or left he had walked through the crowded bar with the holdall swung casually over his shoulder. He had gone quickly and purposefully to his car and put the bag in the boot. Then it was back home to pick up Ian from Mrs Orr. Finally he had crossed the water to England, leaving Belfast behind without even a backward look.

During that journey of less than a hundred miles he had died a thousand times.

Six

Ian stares at his father. The man who is standing in front of him is called Peter Moore. This man Ian knows. For twelve years, ever since his mother's death, Dad has been Ian's only family.

Peter Moore is a widower. He is a self-employed tradesman. He works hard for the money he earns, never cutting corners on a job. He has a strict moral code: give the customer the best service you can. He is equally meticulous about the housework. In what spare time he has, he watches football. Sometimes he reads crime fiction and horror. About half past seven most evenings he falls asleep on the couch, not stirring until gone nine o'clock when he rubs his eyes and wonders where the time has gone. Then he will gruffly ask Ian if he has done all his homework and if he wants some supper.

But there is another presence here, one who goes by the name of Kenny Kincaid, the hazy other half of the good father. This man has robbed a bank and has done God knows what else besides. He has a past. In those yesterdays he has attracted the attention of the Special Branch. He is the ghost who walks in Peter Moore's footsteps. Ian is finding all this hard to take.

'Dad,' Ian says, 'I don't know you.'

Dad is staring back in disbelief at the words. His face is red and a vein is throbbing in his temple.

'Please, Ian, try to understand. Yes, I've done things I wish I hadn't. What do you want from me, son? I can't undo the past.'

'I know,' Ian answers, 'but you can't expect me to feel good about it. It's not like you're telling me you fell down drunk on the stairs or shot a red light, Dad. You stole nearly a quarter of a million pounds!'

In his mind's eye Ian can see Dad walking out of the bank. A man in a balaclava. A man with a gun.

'Come to think of it, you stole it twice – first from the bank then from your mates.'

'Mates?' says Dad. 'Mates? That's a good one! In a dirty war like the one we fought you don't have mates. I'd had enough, that's all. The money gave me a way out.'

'But they were bound to come after you.'

'If I was thinking straight at all, I must have told myself I could stay one step ahead of them. For eleven years I have.'

'And now they're after you again.'

A thought comes into Ian's mind.

'What if they catch up with you?'

Dad's look is all the answer Ian needs.

'Oh God!'

Dad speaks deliberately and with no attempt to pull his punches.

'They've killed before and they will kill again. That gun in Chubby's waistband isn't for show.'

Ian remembers a picture book from infant school in which a boy falls through an apartment building floor by floor. That's the way it is with his life now. Floor by floor his world is giving way under him. The top floor started to crumble when he saw the gun. The one beneath gave way when Dad told him about the money. Now, with this mention of killing, the one below that has just gaped open beneath his feet. Ian has a feeling he's still a long way from the bottom.

'Dad, there's something I have to ask you. I want the truth.'

Dad squints at Ian. He already knows what the question is going to be but he waits anyway.

'What about you? Did you ever kill anybody?'

Dad shakes his head and takes a few steps towards the lock-up.

'Dad?'

Ian watches as his father takes a battered leather briefcase from the lock-up. He isn't sure whether the shake of the head is a yes or merely a gesture of impatience. Ian repeats the question.

'Have you ever killed anyone?'

Dad puts the briefcase on the ground and smashes his fist into the lock-up doors. The doors crash. Flakes of dry paint spiral in the afternoon sunlight. The violence of Dad's reaction takes Ian by surprise. He backs away.

'That's enough!'

The blood falls from Ian's face. Dad sees his reaction and his voice softens.

'We've got to go, son. I wish it was different, but we've no choice.'

Ian nods.

'We'd better get a move on. If they found out about the house, it's a good bet they'll find out about the lock-up. They're both in the same name.'

Ian feels defeated. Without a word he steps through the door. He is about to get changed when he hears Dad's voice.

'Oh no, not now!'

Something in his tone burns deep into Ian.

'What is it?'

Dad is looking up the sliproad towards the one-way system. There is the sound of a car approaching.

'Ian!'

The urgency in Dad's voice is unmistakable. Ian is about to step outside when he sees Dad's hand. He is moving it up and down slowly. The gesture can only mean one thing: stay put.

'It's them, isn't it?'

The hand waves again, a slight, concealed movement that would be unnoticeable from a distance. Ian can hear a roar of a car approaching at speed. A split second later his father hisses an order. Ian can almost hear the effort it takes Dad to keep the naked fear out of his voice.

'Stay where you are and keep your mobile on. I'll be back for you.'

A car door slams. The whine of its engine follows as it reverses away at high speed. Dad executes a handbrake turn and the VW's tyres scream and spin, before gripping and propelling the car forward. Then the two vehicles are gunning down the main road. Confident that he won't be seen, Ian looks outside, but quickly pulls his head in again. Something cuts into his back. That stupid steel comb!

'Dad!'

The Volkswagen is vanishing into the distance pursued by a green saloon.

'Dad . . .'

DS Mark Lomas glances up at the clock. It is a quarter past two. He has been thinking about the statement Annie McDermott gave to the PCs. Lomas reviews the information he has in front of him. Fourteen-year-old Ian Moore was seen being chased along Rochester Avenue by two men. Half an hour later the boy was spotted leaving the shopping centre. A phone call to Ian's school has revealed that he had to go home to change his trousers after an accident. Expected back before lunchtime, he has failed to return to school. Lomas has been trying to contact the boy's father but he has so far drawn a blank. Lomas sighs and turns to his computer. There is plenty more work to be getting on with. It is detailed on the yellow post-it notes stuck to the monitor. Lomas is reading a file when he gets a phone call. He is needed upstairs.

At the viaduct Ian is wondering what to do. Dad has been gone fifteen minutes. What if they have caught up with him? He leans against the lock-up doors. The truth about Dad is crashing round in his skull. His cut hand is aching more than ever. Pain is all around.

'Come on, Dad!'

The last quarter of an hour has been agony as he has stood there willing the VW to come into view. He realises that he hasn't even changed into the new clothes. He is drained, barely able to move.

Stay where you are, Dad said. *I'll be back.*

'But how long am I supposed to stay here? What if those men come back and you don't?'

Ian looks round the lock-up. Other than the van, there is precious little to see, yet the gloomy, windowless unit promises a key to the locked doors in his past. There is a prize to be had, knowledge of who he really is. Ian remembers the briefcase. He picks it up, unfastens the two buckles and opens the catch. It is old so there is no combination. Inside there are papers. There are receipts, bills, that sort of thing, some going back years, but there's nothing which will shed much light on Dad's double life.

Ian is stuffing the wad of papers back in the briefcase when he notices a side-pocket. There is something inside – one of those plastic envelopes you put in ring binders. Inside there is a yellowing newspaper cutting. Ian slides it out. He catches his breath.

'Mum.'

What he has in his hand is a piece from the *Belfast Telegraph*. Ian reads the headline: **Car Bomb Kills Young Mother**.

Car bomb!

'Not a road traffic accident then,' Ian says out loud.

He reads the details:

Police suspect that the device was meant for the dead woman's husband, Kenny Kincaid. Kincaid is an alleged member of the Loyal Ulster Defenders. Royal Ulster Constabulary sources say that the car bomb may be an act of retaliation by a Republican group. The LUD is suspected of involvement in the assassination of community activist Joe McCann last month.

Ian stares at the clipping a long time then takes out his mobile. He hears Dad's voice: *Stay where you are and keep your mobile on.*

Ian shakes his head. Giving a low moan in the back of his throat, he switches off his phone. The fall that began when he saw the stocky man's gun isn't over yet.

DS Lomas knocks and enters the office. He recognises the Assistant Chief Constable.

'Good afternoon, Sir.'

The other man in the room, a burly, grey-haired man in his forties, is unfamiliar.

'Sit down please, Mark,' says the Assistant Chief Constable. 'May I introduce our colleague from Belfast.'

Belfast!

'This is Detective Chief Inspector Ronnie Hagan.'

Lomas steals a glance at the stranger. Odd thing – the two sides of his face don't seem to match.

'So what brings you to our quiet little town?' Lomas asks.

Hagan clears his throat.

'We had intelligence that some of our local hard men were on the move,' he says.

'Terrorism?'

'No. Though these men have roots in paramilitary activity their main interests lie elsewhere. It's some years since they started to diversify, if you get my drift. They cream off some of the profits of their organisation's racketeering. There is the matter of a missing quarter of a million pounds.'

Lomas gives a low whistle. He listens with mounting interest as Hagan tells the story of the Portadown bank raid eleven years ago.

'So what's this got to do with me?' Lomas asks when Hagan has concluded his tale.

'Kenny Kincaid, the man we suspect of taking the money to England, is living right here,' Hagan tells him, 'in your *quiet little town*. He has proved extremely elusive these last few years. He has given us the slip more than once. Then a while back, right out of the blue, he turned up in Belfast. It was his mother's funeral. I've been tracking his whereabouts ever since.'

He rubs his nose.

'Unfortunately, so have some of Kincaid's former accomplices. They were always a couple of steps ahead of me. They found the man who gave Kincaid a new identity here.'

'And he put them on to Kincaid?' Lomas asks.

'Aye, but only after they beat it out of him. He's in intensive care. They've already tried to pay Kincaid a visit. I believe two of your officers were called to an incident.'

Lomas frowns.

'Kincaid? The name doesn't ring a bell.'

'That's because he now goes by the name Peter Moore.'

'Moore!' Lomas exclaims.

The puzzling details of a fourteen-year-old boy's disappearance have suddenly taken on a new significance.

Peter Moore, formerly Kenny Kincaid, has just got out of the blue Volkswagen. Confident that he has given Barr and McClean the slip, he removes something from the glove compartment and shoves it into an inside pocket of his jacket. It is wrapped in a rolled-up plastic bag. He closes the door and walks round to the boot. He takes out the holdall. Everything else he leaves where it is. He plans to come back for the car later. For the time being it is a liability. Barr and McClean have its description and they know the registration number. Risky as it might seem, Moore has decided that, at least for the time being, he is better without it.

He takes a baseball cap from his pocket and pulls it low over his eyes. Walking briskly to the corner of the main road, he switches on his mobile and calls a cab, giving details of a quiet cul-de-sac where he wants to be picked up. He then calls Ian to arrange a place to meet. To his horror, Ian's number is unavailable. He suddenly feels as if he is tumbling into a deep well of fear. As he spirals downwards his memories rush up to meet him.

Seven

Kenny was in the outside lavatory. Nine years old and as lean and bony as a whippet, the young Kenny Kincaid was frozen stiff. The wind was whipping under the rotting wooden door and raising gooseflesh on his thin legs. Though it was July, the day started overcast and cold. Kenny knew what they'd all be saying on the big parade: *Whatever happened to the summers we had years ago? The sun always shone down on the righteous then.*

'Are you not finished in there yet?' shouted his big sister Lou.

'I'll only be a minute,' said Kenny.

The reason he was hiding in there was to wipe off some of the layers of Brylcreem his ma had plastered on his head. Why did she have to ladle the muck on in bucketfuls? It would take an earthquake to move a hair out of place! Kenny looked at all the grease smeared over the squares of newspaper that served as toilet roll in the Kincaid household. Horrible stuff. Hurriedly he flattened his hair with the comb he'd taken from his da's drawer.

'What have you been doing in there all this time?' Lou asked. 'Making your Last Will and Testament?'

Kenny looked at Lou all done up in her Sunday best. She

was still only fourteen but she acted as if she was grown up already.

'I like that!' he retorted. 'Aren't you the one who comes in here sometimes with a library book and sits reading half the day?'

Lou fixed him with a Medusa stare then took a swipe at him, but Kenny ducked under her hand and skipped backwards.

'You'll have to be quicker than that, Lou,' he said. 'Next time you go to the library maybe you should get yourself a book on boxing.'

'You're not too old to get a clip round the ear,' Lou warned him.

Kenny might only have turned nine last birthday but he was nearly as tall as Lou already.

'You don't scare me,' he said.

'No, but your daddy does,' said Lou. 'If you don't clear off in ten seconds I'll tell him how you've been giving me cheek. You just see if I don't.'

Kenny stood with his arms folded.

'Ten, nine, eight . . .' Lou counted.

Kenny had a defiant twinkle in his eye.

'Seven, six, five . . .'

Still he didn't move.

'Four, three, two . . .'

He wondered if Lou was going to do the old one and three-quarters, one and a half.

She didn't.

'One . . .' she said.

'See you later, fat potato!' he said, running into the house.

'Another word out of you, Kenny,' Lou shouted after him, 'and I'll tell Da anyway.'

Inside the house everybody was getting ready for the Twelfth of July parade. In the neighbouring houses the

49

Orangemen had been polishing their flutes and tightening their drums for the march. Kenny's old fella was a member of the Orange Order and the Royal Black Perceptory. The walls were covered with photographs of Kenny's da and his older brother in their British Army uniforms. The Kincaids had a proud history of military service, stretching back to the generation that had fought and died in the Somme. Since he had come out of the Army Kenny's da had had ten years working as a plater at Harland and Wolff.

'Whatever have you done to your hair?' said Ma, licking her fingers and slicking it down.

'Aw, get off!' Kenny protested, but Ma completed the repair job to his hair regardless of his protests.

'If you're going to carry a string on the Lodge banner, then you're going to look presentable,' she told him. 'You do want to hold the string?'

'Yes.'

'Then you leave that hair alone.'

Kenny gave a sigh that came up from the soles of his immaculately polished shoes.

'OK, Ma, I won't touch it again.'

Two hours later Kenny was holding his string. The roar of the Lambeg drums was echoing off the walls. Kenny was fascinated by the Lambeg. Four feet thick and five feet deep, he wondered how a man could even carry the thing never mind play it. The drummers were beating this ancient Ulster weapon with bamboo canes. It set up a terrific racket, a staccato beat that stirred the blood like nothing else he had ever heard. The canes were lashed with leather straps to the drummers' wrists. Kenny had seen a man's wrists slashed right open and his blood spattering the drumhead. He listened to the martial cannonade of the Lambeg drum and felt he was part of a great tradition. He read the banners as they swayed down the terraced streets: *Royal Scarlets, Purple Marksmen, Apron and Blue, Link and Chain.* Way up ahead the Grandmaster of the Lodge, white-gloved, sword in hand, was walking behind a Bible carried on a velvet cushion.

'Hey, Kenny!'

Kenny looked round to see Chubby Barr and Billy McClean dancing along the pavement. He waved.

'I'll see you up at the end of the march,' he told them.

Then they were gone, weaving in and out of the bustling crowds. There were more banners: *Carson's True Blues, Total Temperance.* All the while stern-faced men paraded in black bowler hats and sashes and carried their rolled umbrellas. Kenny watched youths dancing wildly with batons, twirling them and throwing them to impossible heights before catching them as casually as you like.

All of a sudden, amid the beating of the drums and the shrill note of the fifes there was the sound of shouting. Some of the young men who had been accompanying the march were peeling off, whooping with excitement.

'What's going on, Da?' Kenny asked.

'There's a crowd of Taigs up ahead,' Da told him. 'It seems they're hell bent on trouble.'

Then Kenny was craning his neck. He had been raised in a world where there were Prods and Taigs and there were long-standing grievances between them – old as the Antrim hills if some folk were to be believed. There was a line of policemen up ahead. The peelers were holding back the angry Catholic crowd. There was a chase as the odd stone flew at the Protestant marchers.

'I don't know what's wrong with them,' said Da, scowling at the hecklers. 'Why can't they let us march in peace? We didn't come here for trouble. You'd think they owned the streets.'

Kenny saw the Irish tricolour hanging from some of the lamp posts. It was a Catholic street. He wondered if maybe they did own this street, but dismissed the idea immediately. Stupid. The Lodges had always taken this route.

'Step lively,' said Da. 'Walk by them with a straight back and your head held high.'

Kenny did as he was told. He was marching proudly for God and for Ulster. He was about to turn a corner away from the hecklers when he heard a shout that had him wondering.

'Look at you,' the man jeered. 'Think yourself so superior, don't you? Tuppence halfpenny looking down on tuppence, that's all y'are.'

'What does that mean, Da?' Kenny asked as they left the crowd at the road junction behind them. 'What's tuppence halfpenny looking down on tuppence?'

'Take no notice, son,' said Da. 'You'll have to learn to ignore their baiting. You're one of Ulster's young defenders and that's all you need to know.'

Kenny knew what Da told him must be true. Didn't all the songs and banners say so? But the words still had him wondering.

Tuppence halfpenny looking down on tuppence.

Eight

Ian can barely see the High Street ahead of him. His vision is blurred with tears. Oblivious to the shoppers around him he walks straight ahead, the battered briefcase held to his chest. His heart is thumping. From somewhere in the far reaches of his memory, he sees his mother's face swimming up. Where there was only a name there is now a smiling face, features you could almost touch. For the first time in years memories of her break through. He can hear the refrain of the Skye Boat Song and the sound of his own laughter as his mother made up her silly rhymes and tickled him until he thought he would burst.

Then her beautiful face disintegrates and there is fire and debris flying about on his head. All this time he has thought that she was taken from him in a car accident. That was hard enough, trying to come to terms with such a brutal turn of fate. Now it turns out that she was murdered. Dad's enemies killed her. The way Ian is feeling, Dad might as well have done the job himself. He might not have planted the explosive but, sure as eggs is eggs, his actions led to her death, no doubt about that.

'You could have told me, Dad,' he murmurs. 'Surely I deserved that much. She was my mum.'

It was up to Dad what he got himself into, but how could he put his family at risk? How could he leave them in the firing line like that? It was so unfair.

An old woman glances at Ian. She is obviously wondering what is the matter with him, this teenage boy with his bandaged hand and his ill-fitting jeans that bunch up on top of his shoes. Taking no notice Ian walks on, unsure how to feel. Should it be fear of the strangers who have come into his life, misery over his mother's loss or bitterness at his father's betrayal? He is angry that there are no direction posts in this maze of emotions.

What was it he said to Dad? *I don't know who you are.* That is so much more true now that he has read the shocking article from the briefcase. Ian finds himself walking faster and faster, his breathing jerking out of him in shallow gasps and sobs. At the end of the High Street there is a McDonald's. At a loss where to go or what to do next, Ian wanders inside and orders a Fanta. For a while he just stares into space while the busy world spins around him. Then he glances at his watch. It is a quarter to three.

Half a mile across town DS Lomas has just got off the phone.

'I've just got a mobile number for Kincaid. Shall I try him?'

Hagan nods.

'We'll have to get a move on,' he says. 'You don't know Kenny Kincaid. He's a slippery customer. He's given Special Branch and his friends in the LUD the run-around for over a decade. That takes some doing.'

'What I don't understand,' Lomas says, voicing the doubts that have been hanging round in his head, 'is why this issue has become so important all of a sudden. Surely it's old news.'

'The peace process has made this important,' says Hagan. 'I put Barr and McClean away but they're back on the streets. It's lucky for Kenny they were banged up when he came back to Belfast, but the moment they got out they came after him.'

Hagan gives Lomas his lop-sided smile.

'Besides,' he says, 'a quarter of a million pounds is never old news.'

Lomas has a feeling that Hagan isn't telling him everything, but he keeps his suspicions to himself.

'So what sort of a man is this Kincaid?' he asks.

'He is what the Troubles made him,' Hagan answers.

The words surprise Lomas. He expected hostility towards Kincaid.

'Surely you're not serious,' says Lomas. 'He did have a choice, you know.'

'Of course he had a choice,' says Hagan. 'The great majority of the people of the province haven't so much as thrown a stone in anger. Kenny Kincaid's done a lot more than throw a stone, and he knew what he was doing, all right.'

'Exactly,' says Lomas. 'So why are you trying to make excuses for him?'

'I'm not,' Hagan answers. 'I won't excuse terrorism. I've seen too many shattered lives to do that. But I do try to understand the terrorist. You'll find it easier to catch a man if you understand what makes him tick. What has to be remembered is that there's always a man behind the gun. Anywhere normal Kenny Kincaid would have been a model citizen. The truth is, the area of Belfast he was born in isn't normal.'

Lomas gives a half-hearted nod. He can't help feeling that, for some unfathomable reason, Hagan has a soft spot for Kincaid. He is about to say something else when Hagan holds up his hand.

'I think you need to phone him, now.'

Moore, aka Kenny Kincaid, answers the call.

'Ian?' he says hopefully. He has spent the last ten minutes wondering what Ian is doing with his phone switched off.

'Mr Moore?'

Moore frowns.

'Who is this?'

'My name is Detective Sergeant Mark Lomas.'

'Police!'

'That's right, Mr Moore. We have reason to believe that your son has been involved in an incident.'

Moore's heart kicks. So that's what the dead phone means.

Please God, no.

'What kind of incident?'

'A neighbour of yours saw Ian being chased earlier this morning by two men. Part of his school uniform was found later. There were bloodstains.'

Moore relaxes. This is old news.

'Ian left school about half past ten this morning to change his clothes,' Lomas continues. 'He hasn't returned.'

Moore can hear something in the policeman's voice. The phone call isn't really about Ian at all. For some reason this Lomas is fishing for information. Barr and the boys aren't the only ones who are on to him. If the police get their hands on him, he is facing a prison sentence. Moore decides it's time to cut the conversation short. His taxi has just turned into the cul-de-sac.

'We were wondering,' Lomas continues, 'if you'd seen him, Mr Moore.'

Moore climbs into the taxi. He gives a shake of the head and ends the call. He has nothing to say to the police. He leans forward and gives the taxi driver directions. He needs to check if Ian is there or not. Settling back in his seat he thinks about the phone call. No, he has nothing to say to the police. After all, he is no tout.

'What happened?' Hagan demands.

'He hung up,' Lomas says. 'Maybe you should have spoken to him yourself.'

Hagan shakes his head.

'No, not yet. I think it's a bit early to be letting Kenny know I'm in town.'

He smiles.

'If you get another chance to speak to him, just play it the same way. Keep it routine. Let him think it's about his son. Whatever you do, don't let it slip that we know his real identity. Until I tell you otherwise, keep calling him Peter Moore. You've never heard of Kenny Kincaid. Is that clear?'

'Perfectly.'

It is three o'clock when Ian makes his mind up. He finishes his Fanta and walks out of McDonald's. He sees a bin and stops. Taking the cutting about his mother from the brief-case, he folds it twice and shoves it in his pocket. Then he stuffs the briefcase into the bin and walks away. He's half-expecting somebody to challenge him about the briefcase. It isn't the sort of thing a fourteen-year-old boy usually carries and it isn't the sort of thing you put in a bin. He needn't have worried. Nobody has noticed. Jogging across the road, he turns towards school.

Peter Moore is in the public library when the Town Hall clock chimes three o'clock. Before coming in here he checked out the lock-up from a distance. With Chubby and Billy about he doesn't want to put himself in an exposed situation. He could kill Ian for switching off his phone. What is he playing at anyway? Moore is leaning against the wall in the periodicals section, pretending to read a magazine. He isn't interested in the contents, however. It is the view from the library that has brought him in here. From the window he can see the viaduct.

Come on, son. For goodness' sake, show yourself.

Moore is also on the look-out for Billy and Chubby. He would recognise their green Rover immediately. Over and over again, he runs through the possibilities.

Option one: Ian is in the lock-up or over the other side of that wall, waiting the way he was told. That seems doubtful. If he was following instructions he would have his mobile switched on.

Option two: Ian has wandered off for some reason and is on his way back at this very moment. It's possible. Moore has been away a lot longer than he wished.

Option three, one of two possibilities Moore has not wanted to consider: Billy and Chubby already have Ian. That too seems doubtful. Surely they would have called him to use their advantage as a bargaining counter.

Finally there is the other option, maybe even more dangerous than Ian having fallen into the hands of the old gang. What if it has all got too much for him? What if, even now, he is just aimlessly walking the streets?

He is only fourteen, after all, and his world has just fallen apart around him.

Moore knows the feeling. Normally he is good at handling difficult situations. It is a skill he has learned over many years. But this? No, there is no easy way to handle the fact that you have put the life of your only child at risk.

He takes a deep breath. This time he would be a sitting duck. And if Ian isn't there? Surely he would have shown himself by now. Moore closes the magazine and brings his face closer to the window as if it is possible to will his son to come into view.

What do I do? What the hell do I do?

Nine

Kenny Kincaid's education began some weeks after the Twelfth of July march. By education, as he would reflect later, he didn't mean school. The things that nine-year-old Kenny was about to learn they don't teach you in any class- room. One evening he heard Da talking on the doorstep with some of the men from up the street. They were discussing what was happening in Londonderry. Kenny had only the vaguest idea where Londonderry was, but he knew what Londonderry meant. Even its name was argued about. The Protestant people were under siege, so they were, the way they'd been under siege so many times before. It was 1690 all over again. Old battles were being re-fought in the streets and on the barricades.

'They want to shoot and bomb us into a united Ireland,' Da said.

Kenny felt the same kick in his chest as he did when Linfield lost. Shot and bombed into a United Ireland? That sounded bad. A few of us and a lot of them. He had a picture of 'them' in his mind. He saw their faces. They were the crowd who had heckled the march. He imagined them as a tidal wave of emerald green swamping orange Belfast. But aren't there supposed to be more of us? Kenny wondered. Aren't they the few and we the many? How could the Taigs be threatening the Shankill? Aren't the Catholic croppies meant to lie down? Whatever the ins and outs of us and them, Kenny was scared.

'The IRA have started shooting,' Eddie Smith said.

Shooting! Kenny felt a charge of excitement fizz through him. Horror too. How did I miss it? he wondered.

'A bad business,' Da said. 'There was a car showroom on fire last night.'

There, that was something else Kenny had missed. He remembered what Da told him on the big parade: walk by with a straight back and your head held high. But if the IRA was trying to bomb them into a united Ireland, surely you had to do more than walk smartly by? He was still listening to the men when they spotted him sitting on the bottom stair eavesdropping.

'Get inside with you,' Da said, sharply but not angrily. 'This is no business of yours, Kenny.'

Kenny wanted to argue back. He wanted to tell his da that he was Ulster's young defender. Hadn't he held a string on the Lodge banner? Hadn't he kept his head up when the Taigs were hooting and howling at them at that street corner? He wanted to argue back but he didn't, of course. He wasn't going to risk a clip round the ear.

He needn't have worried about missing the trouble. The next night all hell broke loose. That word siege could be heard around the area. There were even fellas making petrol bombs. The smell of burning was in the air. Basins of water were set out and doors were left open for people to run into when things got too hot to handle. Kenny stared in disbelief at what was going on. His ma had always told him they were law-abiding people, but suddenly the law was being made up on the streets. Everybody knew there was a showdown coming.

*It came after dark. The police were exchanging fire with
the IRA, so Da said. The police were shooting Browning
machine guns from their armoured cars. There, that's them,
he said when the metallic rattle echoed down the terraced
streets. As the night wore on there were rumours of people
being shot and others being burned out of their homes.
Kenny wanted to pinch himself to make double sure this
was really happening. It was like cowboys and Indians, only
you didn't get up at the end of the show.*

*Chubby came round, his plump face red with excitement,
saying he had seen tracer bullets flying down the streets like
birds on fire. Billy swore he'd seen his own brother making
petrol bombs. Kenny didn't know whether to believe him or
not. It all seemed a bit too hard to take in.*

*'Go on, then,' Kenny said, annoyed that he'd missed it. 'If
you've seen it done then how do you make one?'*

*Billy was in a showing-off mood. He said you put in a
level of sugar and petrol and a rag soaked with petrol on
top. Kenny didn't know if that was right but it sounded
convincing enough. He would never see Billy McClean in
quite the same light after that.*

*The next events even he couldn't miss. Crowds were
surging up the street. From the front doorstep, which was
as far as his ma would let him go, he could hear their
running feet, following by the smash of glass. Soon after he
would see the glow of fires as houses went up. It was as if the
entire district was in flames. It's a strange thing, the burning
of a town. Though it sickens you right down to the pit of
your stomach it lights a fire inside you too. In spite of
yourself you want to be a part of the rage on the streets.*

*Now, Da didn't hold with throwing petrol bombs and
burning people out of their homes, and you wouldn't catch
him out rioting, but next morning at breakfast he did say
that the IRA had come asking for it. From the way he was*

talking Kenny guessed that there must be thousands of them out there. The emerald green tide was coming closer all the time.

'Are they going to get us, Da?' Kenny asked.

'No,' said Da. 'I won't let them.'

A moment later he added darkly, 'Believe me, if they keep this up, they'll end up getting more than they bargained for.'

For months after the only topic of conversation was the Troubles. Da would sit sipping his tea and muttering about what the British government in Westminster was doing. Wasn't Ulster meant to be a Protestant land for a Protestant people? Though he had little idea quite what they were doing in Westminster, Kenny shared Da's resentment. All he had to say was that they were under siege and Da would pat him on the shoulder and smile.

One day Chubby dared Kenny and Billy to take a different way home. They came across streets of burned-out houses.

'Welcome to Taig town,' said Chubby.

Brickbats littered the streets and there were scorch marks on the walls. Kenny remembered hearing stories about wartime bombing. This was how he imagined it.

'Where did all the people go?' he asked.

'Off to Dublin,' said Chubby with a twinkle in his eye, 'where they belong.'

Billy laughed so Kenny joined in. He knew Dublin belonged to the Taigs but he wanted to know more. Why were they fighting? What were they so angry about? And if they were so in danger of being swamped by that emerald tide, how come it was the Catholics who were running? There was something else he would have to ask Da about.

Da always had this way of making difficult things simple.

One thing he couldn't make simple was the appearance of British troops. Kenny saw them marching down the street with fixed bayonets and steel helmets. Whose side were they on?

'You know what this means,' Chubby said.

'What?'

'It really is a war.'

Kenny watched the soldiers until his ma came and pulled him inside by the ear. He remembered the pictures of the men in his family on the living room walls, all dressed up in their army uniforms. There was a war all right, but it was in their own back yard.

Ten

Ian is ten minutes early for the final bell. Not wanting to hang round the school gates and attract the teachers' attention, he carries on up the street and joins a pensioner couple waiting at a bus stop. The shelter, with its cinema advertisements, gives him cover from which to look out for Vicky.

The terror that has been burning through his veins has subsided a little. His mind is no longer filled with images of the gun in the stocky man's belt. That raw stab of fear has been replaced by a dull, gnawing pain. A darkness has settled inside him, a sense of imminent loss. It isn't just that sometime around eleven o'clock that morning his life jumped the rails. It goes deeper than that. He has seen documentaries about people in crisis. In every case it was their present that was shattered. But Ian has discovered the truth about his past. That too has broken into splinters. It is as if a fastening pin right in the core of his being has been yanked loose. Suddenly everything is flying apart. Nothing is as it seemed.

The security of his home – a lie.

His mother's 'accident' – a lie.

His trust in his father – another lousy lie.

He is angry, disappointed, cut adrift. But he isn't afraid. So much else has happened he just doesn't have time for fear. Maybe he would feel different if he had noticed the hire car parked almost directly opposite. The only vehicle he has been looking out for is a green Rover. In the passenger seat of this other car sits a thin, balding man. His face is so fleshless his head almost reminds you of a skull. The driver has come to Ian's school on the off chance. He didn't expect the boy to turn up. He has just struck lucky.

Peter Moore leaves the library at three-fifteen. Darting glances left and right he jogs down to the lock-up. A ghost walks through him. Ian has gone. There is something else. The place has been turned over. Clothes and scraps of paper have been tossed around the floor. His throat goes dry. I've got everything to do with the money, he thinks, but did I leave anything they could use? Unable to think, he walks briskly to a down-at-heel newsagents and buys the first edition of the evening paper. He flicks through it, all the while peering over the top at the scene in front of him. From the doorway he can see right down the slip road. But there is no movement around the lock-up, no sign of Ian coming back.

'What are you playing at, son? Why'd you turn your phone off?'

Moore checks his watch then closes his eyes. Of course. Three-fifteen. Where else would he be?

'You've gone to see that girl, haven't you?'

He remembers the way Ian was the previous evening. In spite of everything Moore can't help smiling. Ian had been so excited. He was mad about her, this Vicky. He did nothing but talk about her. Moore visualises the look on Ian's face and he remembers the first date with his Tina.

But other memories come and the smile drains from his face.

'That's it Ian, isn't it? You've gone to see Vicky.'

He could just as easily have gone home. Somehow that doesn't fit. No, if Ian has chosen to ignore instructions then he has a reason. It has all got too much for him. He wants to hang on to his old life before he has to leave it behind forever.

'Yes, it's the school all right.'

Moore turns things over in his mind. It will take ten minutes to walk the distance. Even if he is lucky enough to find a taxi here at the edge of the town centre it might not get him there much more quickly. The rush hour builds quickly on a Friday. With a sigh, he sets off on foot. Maybe ditching the VW wasn't such a bright idea. He knows there is more than an even chance that he is walking into an ambush. But this is his son, his only son.

'Vicky! Hey, Vick.'

'Ian!'

Vicky looks him up and down.

'What happened to you?' she asks. 'And what *are* you wearing?'

'It's a long story. Have you got time to listen?'

Vicky waves to her friends. They take the hint and walk on without her. Ian can hear them talking about his appearance.

'I suppose so. Do you want to walk me home?'

As he crosses the road with Vicky a car engine springs to life. Ian doesn't pay attention. The green Rover he would have noticed, but this car isn't green. It's a red Renault Megane. So no problem.

'OK, what's the story? Where did you go? It isn't like you to bunk off.'

'I didn't bunk off.'

Ian is feeling suddenly tongue-tied. All the way over he has been dying to talk and get things off his chest. Now that push has come to shove he doesn't know where to begin.

'So what's happened?'

'There were these men.'

Vicky frowns. Men, what men? Ian has started to wonder what he is doing. Is there really any point dragging her into this shadow world of his, a world of which he himself was totally unaware just hours ago?

'They were at the house. They were . . .'

Ian is finding this harder than he ever expected. Surely one mention of the word *gun* and Vicky will run a mile.

'They were after my dad.'

From the comfort of her settled, suburban life, Vicky can't even imagine the dark undertow that has got Ian in its grip.

'I don't get it.'

'Vicky, they were after him.'

She doesn't dismiss him. She even tries to take a step in his direction.

'Like loan sharks, you mean?'

'Worse.'

When Vicky came up with the idea of loan sharks she was trawling as deeply into the sea of nightmares as her mind would go. What could be worse?

'This is a joke, right?' she asks.

Ian's eyes are still sweeping the street.

'Vicky, this is no joke. I'm in trouble.'

That's when Vicky notices his clumsily bandaged hand.

'Did they hurt you?'

Ian reluctantly takes his eyes off the road and glances at his hand.

'No, not really. Listen, I couldn't hang round at yours for a bit, could I?'

Vicky looks doubtful. She's told Ian about her parents. They're obsessively protective and always hovering when she has a friend home, especially a male friend.

Big Brother is watching you.

'Just for half an hour, Vicky. Please. I need time to think.'

'OK, half an hour. I'll tell Mum we're doing our homework together.'

'Thanks, Vick.'

When they turn the corner the skull-headed man lets himself out of the car. He starts to follow the couple on foot. The driver pulls away slowly. He is a tall, gaunt man in a leather jacket. A wolfman.

By the time Peter Moore comes panting up to the school gates there are only a handful of stragglers making their way through. He wonders whether to wait then rejects the idea. If, for any reason, Vicky were still inside then Ian would be standing right here waiting for her. No, they're long gone.

Moore thinks of Ian with his girl and he aches inside. He remembers the day his Tina died. He'd walked to the shop to get a pint of milk. Tina had said something as he left but he didn't quite catch it. He passed his car, pausing for a moment to look at it. After the McCann hit he knew he was a target for retaliation. He had a well-worn routine for dealing with such a possibility. He would drop his car keys. When he knelt down to retrieve them he would steal a glance at the underside of the vehicle, just in case there was a device. The search would have to wait till later. Milk was the priority. He was at the counter paying for the milk when her words fizzed to life in his head. She was going to move the car. The tyre was up on the kerb and it could cause damage.

Standing outside the school gates, Peter Moore relives that moment. He is Kenny Kincaid turning, making for the door, knowing he has to stop his wife turning the ignition key. She doesn't know a thing about the McCann hit. It is all happening again in slow motion, like the highlights of a major sporting event. He runs, sees her reaching for the door. He yells her name. She smiles cheerfully, thinking he is running for the devilment of it, then waves and slips into the driver's seat.

'Tina, get out of there!'

Kincaid knows it is no more than an outside chance that the car is booby-trapped, but an outside chance is still a chance. Outside chances have been taking lives through all the years of the Troubles.

'Tina!'

The engine turns and Kenny Kincaid's world spins off its axis and rolls into Hell. Reality cracks like a broken mirror. In a fireflash all the sound is sucked out of the street. Kenny Kincaid is thrown back. By the time his body crumples to the ground he is lying, numbed by loss, inside a tunnel of silence. A dull, rolling, soundless blanket envelops him.

'Tina!'

Peter Moore's eyes prickle with the tragedy of Kenny Kincaid.

'I've lost my wife,' he says grimly. 'I won't lose my son.'

Eleven

Kenny Kincaid was mopping up the last of the runny egg yolk with his soda bread. He was thirteen years old. His mother cleared away his plate. She paused at the sink, plate in hand.

'What are you doing with yourself today?'

She knew she was hardly likely to get a worthwhile answer but she asked anyway. It's what mothers do.

'The usual. We'll be going to the game. Chubby and Billy are calling for me.'

Ma stiffened. There was a time when she liked having the boys round the house. That all changed with the Troubles. Billy she could handle. He was quiet, sometimes disturbingly so, a lean, brooding beanpole of a boy, but he wouldn't give you any trouble, not unless Chubby was with him. No, Chubby was the one. He was a real tough, heavily built and loud. Nobody teased him on account of his size – not if they wanted to go home with the same number of teeth they came out with.

'You will be careful,' Ma said.

'What's to be careful about?' Kenny asked.

Ma looked at him with his collar-length hair and his half-mast blue jeans and bovver boots and wondered where her

71

bright, eager-to-please little boy had gone. It was a daft question, of course. Her little lad had gone down to Hell like the rest of this town. Respect and decency had been shot to pieces by baton rounds and bullets. Violence and retribution hung round the place like a pair of vultures. The Troubles had stolen all the wee boys' childhoods.

What's to be careful about? She sighed. 'Nothing,' she said.

What she meant was everything.

The boys were walking near the head of the crowd. Their tartan scarves were tied round their wrists. When they came past the Catholic flats at the bottom of the road there was a crowd out shouting insults. The boys responded by hurling abuse back. Some were chanting the score. The Blues had won. Chubby, as ever, led the way. He pushed himself to the front, raising both hands above his head and calling the youths opposite forward.

'What's your problem?' he shouted when they halted at the road junction. 'Too scared to come out of your hidey-holes? What's the matter? Going to wet your wee panties, are you?'

All the boys around him were egging him on. Their opponents were giving as good as they got, especially a nasty piece of work by the name of Joe McCann, but Chubby carried on oblivious to their battle-cries. He was quite the big man, taunting the Taigs. Soon he was treating them to a raucous and none-too-tuneful rendition of 'The Sash my Father Wore'. The opposition just roared and whistled and sang their own anthems until the football crowd peeled away.

'Sure,' said Kenny, clapping Chubby on the back. 'You gave them what for.'

*

Da was out the front of the house painting the window frames when he saw Kenny rolling up the street with his pals. Like Ma, he wondered where his wee boy had gone. He hardly recognised this young tearaway. If you come across trouble you just walk on by with a straight back, he'd told young Kenny once. Be proud and look away. Let the insults roll right off you. Walking on a parade was one thing, but going out with your fists up, looking for trouble was another.

Kenny wasn't inclined to walk past any kind of trouble these days. Some of his friends were already hanging round the militias being set up to defend the area. Kenny wanted to be in there, trading punches with the best of them, only the time for fistfights was at an end. It was guns now, and bombs. Da didn't quite know where things had gone wrong, but gone wrong they had.

'Did you win?' Da asked.

'What do you think?'

That was all the answer he got. Chubby said something and Kenny and Billy brayed like a pair of donkeys. Da didn't ask what was so funny. He didn't think it would make him laugh.

'I hope you've been behaving yourselves,' he said.

This set off another gale of laughter, as if there was anything funny about behaving yourself.

'We always do,' Kenny said, digging Chubby in the ribs.

Da watched them jog off down the street. He remembered when he used to play in the street himself. If the policeman caught you disturbing the men sleeping after a night shift, you ran. These days it was the peelers who ran.

Everybody ran the day Sam Mitchell's bar went up. Kenny was with Chubby and Billy when they heard the explosion. They'd been sitting on top of a wall, throwing stones at

73

a line of bottles, when there was an ear-shattering explosion.

'What was that?' Chubby gasped, rolling off the wall.

'It sounds like half the Shankill's gone up,' said Kenny.

As usual Billy just gave them a glance and followed them along the road.

'What's happened?' Chubby asked a man who was reeling towards them as if he was drunk.

The man's face was grimy with dust. He looked at the boys for a moment then spoke with a voice that seemed to come from far away.

'Go round that corner and you'll soon see.'

Once round the corner they saw what he meant. People were staggering through a thick, rolling cloud of dust. They were coughing and retching. Their skin was caked with particles of brick and mortar. Their eyes were windows of shock and bewilderment in the grey masks of their faces. There was one word on everybody's lips: bomb.

'The scum!' somebody was crying. 'The lousy, murdering scum!'

In his mind's eye Kenny saw the crowd of youths outside the flats, the mob who had hurled abuse at the parade when he was a wee boy. That's where the bombers were bred, among those screaming mouths and those staring eyes. He wanted to rip the hearts out of them, those shrieking IRA demons.

It wasn't like Chubby to go quiet, but he went quiet that Saturday evening. He looked at the rubble and the bodies being carried out by the ambulance crews and he was shocked to silence.

'Jeez!' Chubby said.

That's what attracted the policeman.

'Get away, boys,' he said, his voice as splintered as the glass from Mitchell's bar. 'This is no place for you. Go

home, will you? Didn't you understand? People are dead in there.'

Dead!

At that Chubby and Kenny ran and Billy came pounding after them. They were streets away before they stopped.

'Did you hear what he said?' Chubby panted. 'There are people dead under that rubble.'

'It's not right,' Kenny said. 'Those that planted the bomb are the ones who should be dead.'

He remembered that day on the parade when he and his da had marched past the taunting mob. Then the thought of McCann and his crowd of Taigs ignited a blazing anger in Kenny Kincaid. Until the explosion he had watched the hard men from afar, faces masked and eyes hidden behind sunglasses as they built their barricades. He had been both fascinated and unnerved. Now he knew he wanted to be one of them – a soldier fighting for the Loyalist people of Belfast.

After that day Kenny Kincaid's life would never be quite the same again.

Twelve

About the same time Peter Moore starts walking away from the school gates, Ian and Vicky are crossing the main road near her home.

'So what's this trouble exactly?' Vicky asks. 'Or can't you tell me?'

Ian shrugs. Knowing his luck, the truth would go down like a lead balloon.

'I'd better not say anything,' he answers miserably. 'But you've got to believe me, it's bad.'

Vicky gives him an enquiring glance. If this is some kind of joke then the punch line is a long time coming.

'Just humour me, eh, Vick?' he says, his gaze falling away from her face. 'Right now I need a friend.'

A friend he's got, as Vicky shows him with a sympathetic smile, but close by there is unwanted company in the shape of Hugh McCullough. Lean and balding, pale as a flake of cod, McCullough doesn't stand out on the street. To all intents and purposes he is just another middle-aged man on his way home from work. He crosses the road some thirty yards behind Ian and Vicky and follows them at an even pace. From time to time he glances behind at the

76

red hire car parked in a side street opposite. The wolfman Billy McClean is watching.

'Have you fallen out with your old man or something?' Vicky asks. 'Is that what all this is about?'

'It's part of it,' Ian admits.

Vicky smiles. She looks pleased with herself, as if she has just seen through his tall story. She wants there to be a simple explanation for Ian's tale of mystery. She doesn't want his life to be engulfed in darkness. Darkness is something that should be saved for nameless lives on the evening news.

'It isn't the whole story though,' he says, wrenching her away from the comfort zone. 'Dad's in way over his head. He did something . . . terrible.'

The smile lingers on Vicky's lips. She looks at him uncertainly, still not quite sure whether to take him seriously.

'Listen, Ian,' she says, coming to a stop and turning to look at him. 'I don't mean to be funny, but when we get to mine not a word of this. You'll freak Mum out completely.'

'I'll behave myself,' says Ian. 'I just need a few moments.'

Vicky squeezes his arm.

'You've got them.'

Thirty yards behind them Hugh McCullough is biding his time. He is poised to move the moment Ian says goodbye to Vicky. There is no point making things complicated by involving the cute little blonde in their business.

Come on, dump the girl!

He is aware of Billy McClean looking on over the rim of the steering wheel.

Say goodbye to her, will you? Give us all a break.

But Ian has no intention of saying goodbye. He and the

girl carry on walking to the street corner and turn left. McCullough glances across the road at McClean, then follows. He hears the Megane's engine purr into life. When McCullough comes to the corner he sees Ian and the girl turning left again. Off the main road the streets are quieter. McCullough looks around at the suburban respectability, all flower beds and manicured lawns. Maybe this is the time to make his move. So what if the girl sees them take Kenny's son? It's not as if she will have a clue what's happening. By the time the peelers get a whiff of what's really going on they'll have prised the cash out of Kenny Kincaid's sticky paws. McCullough sees the Megane pulling round the corner and mouths a question.

Now?

McClean nods impatiently and McCullough makes his move.

'Say as little as possible,' Vicky tells Ian. 'Leave the talking to me. Just go along with whatever I say.'

Ian nods. He hears footsteps behind him and turns round. He sees the balding man approaching and, for a moment, anxiety buzzes through him. Vicky is still fumbling for her key when her mother opens the door.

'You're late, aren't you, Vicky?' says Mrs Shaw.

Vicky frowns. 'Am I?'

She glances at her watch.

'Mum, it's only a few minutes. You've got to cut me some slack once in a while.'

Mrs Shaw shifts her gaze to Ian. He sees the troubled look which, he suspects, is never far away.

'And this is . . . ?'

'Oh, surely you remember Ian. He walked me home from bowling last week. We're in the same set. We're going to do our homework together.'

Ian is aware of Mrs Shaw looking him over. The troubled look never leaves her face. Her eyes fasten on the clumsily-bandaged hand. Instinctively he slips his hand behind his back.

'Did you have an accident, Ian?' Mrs Shaw asks.

'Oh, yes. I trapped it in a door this morning.'

Sometimes lies are so much easier than the truth.

'Not in school uniform today?'

'No,' says Ian, thinking on his feet while hoping Vicky won't drop him in it. 'I've had the day off.'

'Who did that bandage?'

Ian shrugs, knowing he's being less than convincing.

'Dad, I think. Yes, Dad.'

Vicky's seen the traffic lights in her mother's mind change from amber to red. She interrupts.

'So can I invite him in, Mum?' she asks. 'We'll only be an hour.'

'I suppose so,' says Mrs Shaw, stepping aside reluctantly to admit them. There is a quiver of uncertainty in her voice. 'But I mean an hour. You've got your gymnastics later and you need to get changed.'

Vicky smiles.

'Thanks, Mum.'

Ian sees Hugh McCullough carry on up the street. You're worrying about nothing, he thinks. No danger there.

Not wanting to alert the boy to his presence, McCullough keeps walking. Snatching Ian when there's just the girl about is one thing. Doing it with the woman – and possibly a husband – watching is another matter. McCullough walks to the end of the road, waits for the red Megane and leans through the passenger window.

'What do you reckon, Bill?' he asks.

'We wait,' says McClean. 'It's a quiet neighbourhood. We won't get a better chance.'

McCullough nods, opens the passenger door and slides in. McClean adjusts his rear-view mirror and watches the house.

Even in the apparent safety of Vicky's front room, Ian can't settle. He is sitting on the edge of his chair, darting his eyes at the front window. His roughly-bandaged right hand picks compulsively at the material of his jeans.

'You really are worried about something, aren't you?' says Vicky.

Ian nods.

'Let's talk about something else though,' he says.

He has made his mind up. There is no way he can confide in Vicky. It would do no good and it would probably be the end of any relationship. He can just imagine the look on Mrs Shaw's face if she knew the truth. No, better to change the subject entirely.

'If you like,' says Vicky.

'So what did I miss today?' Ian asks. 'What's the latest goss? Did Jenny knock Gareth back, the way I said?'

'You're joking, aren't you?' says Vicky, her face lighting up. 'Didn't you see them outside school? She was snogging the gob off him.'

'Never!'

'Straight up. They're definitely an item.'

While Ian is finding out that his best friend Gareth has just copped off with the gorgeous Jenny Latham, Peter Moore is coming down the main road, not two minutes' walk away. The street lamps are casting an amber glow on the darkening streets, but nothing can lift the gloom in his mind.

'She lives round here somewhere,' he says out loud. 'Why the hell didn't I ever ask where?'

Ian walked her home one night last week. What did he say? Halfway down Hunger Hill, by the chippy. Moore glances across the road at the Chinese chippy. The lights are on, a bleary yellow glow spilling on to the pavement. This is it, all right, but what was the name of her road? Come on, man, think! The address just won't come. Moore tries Ian's phone again but there is still no answer.

Thirteen

Kenny came panting up to the street corner. His ma had made him late, telling him to do both lots of homework. He groaned inwardly. The boys would think he'd bottled out. And it was his idea to join the Young Defenders in the first place. He'd talked about little else since Sam Mitchell's bar went up. It was two years since the explosion and ever since Ma and Da Kincaid had been fighting a rearguard action to keep Kenny out of trouble.

'Are you looking for Jimmy Barr?' a reedy, singsong voice asked.

Kenny looked around. It was Tina Rea. Tina was only twelve, three years younger than Kenny, but he knew she had a powerful crush on him. The way she hung round him it didn't take ESP to work it out.

'Yes. Why? Have you seen him?'

'I saw them going in the back door of Sam Mitchell's bar,' Tina told him, 'not half an hour ago.'

Mitchell's Bar had been rebuilt completely since the bombing a few years back. The cage protecting the front door and the red hand painted over the lintel served notice that this establishment was in no mood to give in to Fenian IRA bombers.

'They've already gone?' said Kenny. 'Are you sure about this?'

'Sure as I'm standing here talking to you,' said Tina.

She'd taken a step closer, as if to tell Kenny she deserved a reward for the information. He chose to reach out his hand and tousle her mop of dark hair. It was a gesture that was calculated to annoy her and get her off his back. There she was, Tina Rea, longing with all her heart to be his girl and he was treating her like a little kid. It was just about the worst insult he could have invented. Kenny saw her pout of irritation and chuckled to himself all the way to Sam Mitchell's Bar.

Kids!

At the back door of the bar he knocked twice and waited. It didn't do to show impatience. When he turned round he found himself looking up at Andy Craig, eighteen stone of Defender muscle.

'Are you the one that knocked?' Craig asked, knuckle-hard voice working its way up from the bottom of his boots.

'I'm with Chub– I'm with Jimmy Barr and Billy McClean.'

'Funny – they didn't say anything.'

'Well, I am. So can I come in then?'

'Down the steps,' said Craig, stepping to one side to let him pass.

Kenny jogged down the dark stairwell and walked into a cellar lit by a single, unshaded lightbulb. He was aware that he had left more than the light of day behind. This musty basement world reminded him of the old spy films they showed on TV.

Billy was sitting on a chair on the other side of the room.

'Where's Chubby?' Kenny asked, taking a seat next to Billy.

'In there.'

Billy was pointing in the direction of a second room. The door was closed.

'He's getting sworn in to the Young Defenders, just like we said.'

'You came without me?'

'We thought you'd lost interest,' Billy said, without even looking at Kenny.

'How's that?' Kenny said, outraged. 'Wasn't I the one who suggested it in the first place?'

'Your ma said you were too busy with your books. Turning into a bit of a teacher's pet, aren't you?'

'No,' said Kenny.

It was obvious what Billy meant. Kenny had done really well in his exams. When the results came through Mr Campbell fairly glowed with pleasure. The boy had come good in the end.

'That's not what your ma says,' Billy snorted. 'She told my ould girl you might even be going off to university.'

Kenny still liked the sound of that, university, but just then he had bigger fish to fry.

'Take no notice of her,' he said fiercely. 'It's all hot air. You know how mothers are. I'm leaving this summer, same as you.'

He delivered the line as off-handedly as he could. Kenny Kincaid was going to fight for God and Ulster. But for all the fire in his belly he couldn't help but wonder what he was giving up. Fighting for his people wasn't the only dream he had.

'What would I be doing with all that studying?' he said, with as much conviction as he could muster.

Billy eyed Kenny suspiciously, then grinned.

'So it's a tale she was spinning?'

'Of course it was. You don't think I'd break the old gang

up over a few exams, do you? If girls can't split us up then exams surely won't.'

Billy gave a quick shake of the head. Relief broke through the mask of contempt. 'We were worried for a while, don't you know?'

'No need to be,' said Kenny. 'When have I ever let you down?'

Billy gave Kenny a playful punch on the arm.

'Never.'

When it was Kenny's turn to be sworn in, he was led into a small room. On the bare table in front of him there was a Union Jack with a Bible on it. Two burly men in combat jackets asked him a series of questions.

Would he defend God and Ulster?

He would.

Would he do all in his power to defend his community?

He would.

Would he obey the orders of his commanding officer without question?

He would.

When Kenny left the room to join Chubby and Billy he felt a pang of regret. Mum would be so disappointed that he was leaving school. Chubby and Billy clapped their hands on his back and shoulders. The regret only lasted a moment.

Fourteen

Vicky goes into the kitchen to fetch a couple of Cokes from the fridge. Still on edge from the events of the day, Ian gets up and walks over to the window. He looks out on to the street. It isn't even five o'clock but night has fallen like an old coat. If he were to crane his neck over to the left a little he might just glimpse the wing of the red Megane through the murk and wonder. But he doesn't look. He doesn't see. He is still at the window when he hears Vicky and her mother in the kitchen.

'Vicky,' Mrs Shaw is saying, 'are you sure you know what you're doing?'

'What do you mean?'

'You know what I mean. This boy . . .'

Vicky interrupts. 'His name is Ian.'

'OK, Ian. What do you know about him?'

'He's in my class at school. What's to know?'

Impatience catches in Mrs Shaw's voice.

'I'll tell you what, young lady. Have you actually taken a good look at him? His clothes don't fit. He's like a cat on hot bricks all the time. Then there's that bandage. I don't care what he says, his dad didn't do that. The state of it!'

'What are you saying?'

'Vicky . . .'

Mrs Shaw is searching for the words.

'He isn't on drugs or anything, is he?'

Vicky is outraged.

'Don't be ridiculous!'

'Vicky, you've got to admit–'

'Mum, I don't have to admit anything. He's a friend. There's nothing wrong with him.'

Vicky sounds tearful.

'That's it,' Ian says to himself. 'This has gone on long enough.'

He steps into the hallway just in time to see Vicky walking out on her mother. Seeing Ian standing there, Mrs Shaw gives up her pursuit. For a moment the three of them just look at each other.

'I'm going,' Ian says.

'No, Ian, don't!'

'It's been an hour,' he tells her. 'I'd better be off.'

'You overheard, didn't you?'

Vicky looks accusingly at her mother.

'Stay,' says Vicky. 'It doesn't matter what she says.'

Ian glances at Mrs Shaw.

'Yes,' he replies, 'it does. I don't want to cause any trouble.'

'You're not,' Vicky cries. 'Tell him, Mum.'

But Mrs Shaw looks away.

'I do think it's for the best,' she says, her voice as cold and sharp as an ice crystal.

Vicky is about to protest again, but Mrs Shaw raises a hand.

'Victoria,' she says coldly, 'don't make this any worse than it already is. I think you've said quite enough.'

Her eyes flick back to Ian.

'You're right, Ian. It's time to go.'

Up the street, McClean nudges McCullough, who is lying back in the passenger seat with his eyes closed.

'This is it,' he says. 'The front door's just opened.'

McCullough twists round to see the three figures caught in the light from the hall. 'There he is.'

He goes to get out but McClean restrains him.

'Wait till they close the front door. We don't want any witnesses.'

They only have to wait for a moment. As soon as Ian is through the front gate Mrs Shaw pulls Vicky back inside. With a brief glance back, Ian starts towards the main road.

'OK,' McClean says. 'Go!'

Ian sees the skull-headed man first. But it isn't until he sees the driver of the Megane as it moves off that he is alerted to the danger.

The wolfman!

The realisation that they've caught up with him rips through his soul. It slams the breath from him. For a second he is rooted to the spot. Then he's running again, his feet pounding the deserted pavement. He is running, but it isn't like this morning. Hard as he pushes himself, desperately as he sprints for the main road, something has gone since that first sighting of the gun – a self-belief, a conviction that he can beat them. All that running he did, all that hiding, the theft of the clothes – and here they are again. What's more, it isn't just the two of them this time. That skull-headed man – he's new. So there have got to be at least three men on Dad's trail. If only, Ian thinks, if only I hadn't walked away like that. He can feel the mobile phone in his pocket. Why didn't I at least call to say I was OK?

Somehow I've got to lose them and raise the alarm.

But losing them is easier said than done. Ian can see the

main road up ahead but Skullhead is closing and the red Megane has just roared ahead. There's no way out.

Peter Moore is in the lounge bar of the Red Lion, not a quarter of a mile away. He has phoned Ian several times. He has even phoned home twice just in case, but there was no answer.

'Ian, where the hell are you?'

Then he has an idea. Of course! Gareth might know where the girl lives. Moore finds the number in his directory. Gather yourself, he thinks. Try not to sound agitated. Calm. Nothing out of the ordinary. Just a father trying to track down his son.

'Hello?'

It's a woman's voice.

'Hi there, Mrs Evans,' he says, doing his best to sound casual. 'It's Ian's dad. I'm trying to track down that boy of mine. That's right, he's got his mobile switched off. Menaces, aren't they?'

He listens to Mrs Evans for a few moments.

'No, I know he isn't with Gareth. I think he's visiting this girl he's keen on – Vicky. You wouldn't have her number, would you?'

He can hear Mrs Evans calling up the stairs. Maybe twenty seconds later Gareth picks up the phone. He asks where Ian got to after going home but Moore manages to field it.

'Do you have her number then?' he asks.

'Sorry, Mr Moore,' he says, 'I haven't got it. I might be able to get hold of it for you, though. Can I make a call and phone you back?'

Moore feels a surge of optimism.

'Would you mind? Here, I'll give you my mobile number.'

'OK,' Gareth says. 'I won't be a minute.'

The Megane slews across the road in front of Ian and McClean jumps out to join the chase.

'Stop!' he says. 'We don't mean you any harm.'

Ian isn't listening. All he sees is danger. He flees into the garden of the corner house. He is instantly aware of the houseowner tugging at the net curtains – an Englishman defending his castle.

'I know what you're after!' Ian yells. 'I know about the money!'

Skullhead and Wolfman stop for a beat then make a lunge for him. He jumps back but not quickly enough. Wolfman succeeds in grabbing a handful of his sleeve, spinning him round.

'You've led us a merry chase,' snarls McClean. 'Now do as you're told and get in the car.'

Ian is led struggling to the car when an elderly man opens the front door of the house.

'What's going on here?' he asks.

His voice is shrill with fright.

'None of your business,' snaps McCullough.

McClean darts an angry glare at him and tries to retrieve the situation. Why draw attention to themselves?'

'Nothing to worry about,' he says, digging his fingers into the flesh of Ian's arm. 'This is my nephew. He's done a runner from home. You know what teenagers are like.'

The houseowner doesn't look convinced. Ian takes advantage of his obvious doubt.

'Don't believe them!' he cries. 'I don't know them!'

McClean tightens his grip.

'Now don't be stupid, Ian,' he says, gouging his fingers into the flesh of the boy's arm. 'Don't go making up stories again.'

Ian is struggling but he can't break free.

'Please,' he begs, turning pleading eyes on the elderly man. 'You know this isn't right. Do something.'

The houseowner looks on helplessly. He knows there is nothing he can do against the pair.

'Please don't hurt the lad,' he says feebly.

'Don't worry,' McClean pants. 'We're returning him to his parents, that's all.'

Before Ian can say another word the two men drag him across the front lawn, lead him struggling to the car and bundle him into the back seat.

Moore's mobile rings.

'Hello?'

'It's me, Gareth. I couldn't get the phone number but I've found Vicky's address.'

'Don't worry,' says Moore. 'It's the address I want.'

Gareth is still wondering about Ian's absence from school.

'Are you sure everything's all right?' he asks.

'Of course. Why wouldn't it be?'

'Just wondering,' says Gareth. 'Anyway, here's the address.'

DS Mark Lomas takes an internal phone call. When he hangs up he glances at Ronnie Hagan.

'Something for us?' asks Hagan.

'Might be,' says Lomas. 'Sarge has just taken a call from an elderly gentleman down Hunger Hill. He has a report of a young lad being bundled into a car by two men. They said he was a relative, but it didn't sound kosher.'

'Anything else?'

'Yes,' says Lomas. 'The men had Irish accents.'

*

McCullough sits in the back with Ian while McClean drives away. It has started to spit with rain and the wipers are on intermittent, flicking away the heavy drops.

'Well,' says McClean, 'you're a chip off the old block, I'll give you that. Hours we've been looking for you. You're a Kincaid, all right.'

'You're not going to get my dad!' Ian yells.

'Ah, now that's where you're wrong,' says McCullough, speaking for the first time. 'We're going to get your da all right, and we're going to get the money too. So be a good lad and stop fighting the inevitable.'

Ian makes an effort at defiance.

'I'll tell him not to come.'

The two men laugh.

'And you think he's going to listen?' says McCullough. 'No, not when we've got his boy. The moment he knows we've got you he'll come running.'

'Then I won't tell you his number,' says Ian.

'No need,' says McClean. He holds up a card.

'We found this in a newsagent's window.'

Ian reads the card:

General tradesman – household repairs.
Work done to the highest standard.
Call Peter Moore.
078955 27707

His heart sinks.

Ten minutes later Peter Moore is walking away from Vicky Shaw's house with a flea in his ear. Ian has obviously done something to upset the mother. Not that Moore cares who Ian has upset – he just wants to know where he is. He pauses by the corner house. There are skid marks in the road. For a moment Moore wonders. He looks up and down the street, but it is deserted.

'Where are you, Ian?' he says.

He swallows hard. He feels utterly helpless. He is closer to tears than at any time since Tina died.

'Where in God's name are you, son?'

Fifteen

It was five years since Kenny Kincaid had joined the Young Defenders. He was twenty but there was a look about him. He could be five, ten years older. There was something in his eyes, the set of his jaw. That Bible on the Union Jack, that oath of allegiance – they had changed his life. His days had been a routine of marches, meetings and parades, but now he was called on to fight for God and Ulster. He had built roadblocks. He had kept watch at junctions in bush hat, combat jacket and dark glasses. He had doled out beatings, both to Taigs who had wandered out of their area and Prods who had forgotten the rules of their own community. He had left school early, just the way he told Billy, and started work with Da. Ma had fretted over his decision, of course, but there was no going back. Now he was waiting for the call to arms, when he would be Ulster's true defender.

There was money in his pocket. He liked a pint but he didn't drink heavily, not the way Billy and Chubby did. They were halfway to pickling their vital organs.

Sometimes Kenny heard how such and such a wee girl from round the corner had gone off to university or that so-and-so's boy was going to train as a teacher and he felt a pang. It wasn't jealousy exactly, more loss. It didn't last long though, because Billy and Chubby would always be round to drag him off and show him a good time. Kenny had made his bed and now he had to lie in it. He looked in the mirror and straightened his tie. He was doing all right but he was only living half the life he could have done. He felt an emptiness. There was part of him that was lying mothballed and unused inside.

'You're a fool to yourself, Kenny,' he told the mirror.

But there was no time to continue the conversation with his reflection because Lou came knocking on the bathroom door, the way she came knocking years ago on the outside toilet door. She was no gawky teenager now though. It was Lou's wedding day. She'd got herself a peeler – a serious young fellow four years in the Royal Ulster Constabulary. It was dangerous work being a police officer in the province. They were a target for the IRA. Even the Loyalist community weren't happy. Chubby said it was a Prod police force, so why didn't they act like it? Still, for all the danger and the aggro, at least the money was good. More to the point, Lou seemed genuinely in love with her peeler.

'Aren't you finished yet?' she complained. 'Whose day is it anyway, Kenny?'

He opened the door and put his hands on her shoulders.

'It's yours, Lou,' he said. 'And by the way, you're looking beautiful.'

As he walked away he was aware of her staring after him. For once in her life she was lost for words. Kenny smiled. That sure shut her up.

'There you are, Kenny,' Ma said. 'You should wear a suit more often. See how sharp you look. You're such a handsome young man.'

'Don't tell me,' said Kenny. 'You're looking to marry me off again.'

He knew how Ma's mind worked. Her oldest, Robert, had been married for eight years. Lou had got herself a nice young fella. That was two of her three kids married off, so it was high time Kenny got himself a girl.

'There's plenty of time for settling down later,' he told her. 'Right now I'm too busy having fun.'

Ma shook her head. The girls liked Kenny. He never had any difficulty getting a date on a Saturday night. But there was nobody special, nobody who was going to wear his ring.

'Maybe you're right,' said Ma, 'but don't you be leaving it too long. I'd like to see all the family settled and I'm not getting any younger.'

Kenny took her hands.

'Ma,' he said, 'you're invincible. You'll outlive us all.'

The photographer was trying to martial the wedding guests into some sort of order when Kenny noticed a group of girls watching from the road.

'Who's that?' he whispered to Chubby.

'Which one are you looking at?'

'There. White top and black skirt. Mane of black hair.'

'You mean you don't remember her?'

Kenny reached deep into his memory.

'No.'

Then the penny dropped.

'You mean to tell me that's Tina Rea?'

A nod.

'That skinny wee thing!'

There was nothing skinny or wee about her now.

'The very same.'

'Didn't somebody tell me they'd emigrated?' Kenny asked.

'Yes, about four years ago. They went to Canada, I think. They came back a couple of weeks ago.'

96

Kenny stared and Tina met his eye.

'You won't believe I chased her away once,' Kenny said. 'Years ago. She was just a wee girl with a crush on me. She couldn't have been more than twelve or thirteen.'

Chubby glanced at Tina and saw her friends nudging her and giggling.

'I'll bet you won't be chasing her away now.'

At the first opportunity, Kenny slipped away but there was no sign of Tina. He jogged to the end of the road and looked right and left. Disappointed, he dug his hands deep in his trouser pockets and started to walk back to the church.

'Looking for somebody?'

The voice came from behind him.

Kenny spun round.

'Tina!'

She stepped out from an alley.

'You remember me then?'

'Of course I do. You're back from Canada then?'

Tina reached out her arms as if confirming her presence.

'Looks like it.'

'So it didn't work out over there?'

'No,' said Tina. 'It worked out just fine. Mum wanted to come back, that's all. She missed Belfast.'

'And you?'

A smile lit up Tina's face.

'I missed some things.'

'Maybe we could meet up later for a drink,' Kenny said. 'Then you could tell me what you missed.'

'I don't mind meeting you,' Tina said, 'but the drink's out. I'm still only seventeen.'

'You could pass for eighteen,' Kenny told her.

'Yes, and Da would have a fit. He doesn't hold with drink at the best of times, never mind under-age drinking.'

For a while Kenny didn't know what to say.

'Can I call for you when I'm finished here?' he said eventually. 'Where are you living now?'

Tina told him the address.

'Very nice. It's a wonder you still want to know us down here.'

'I'll always want to know you,' said Tina.

And the look she gave him took his breath away.

Sixteen

Hagan is leaning over Lomas's shoulder, reading his scribbled notes.

'So what's the score?' Hagan asks when Lomas puts down the phone.

'The uniformed boys have been making a few house calls,' Lomas explains.

'And?'

'Ian Moore has a friend called Gareth Evans. It seems Kincaid – I mean Moore . . .' Lomas gives Hagan a sidelong glance. The Ulsterman's crooked face rarely betrays a flicker of emotion. What are you thinking? Lomas wonders.

'Peter Moore phoned Gareth Evans about half an hour ago. He wanted the address of his son's girlfriend.'

'So what are we waiting for?' Hagan asks, shrugging on his coat.

'It's already been followed up,' Lomas tells him. 'Ian Moore has already left the house. The girlfriend's mother doesn't like him.' He frowns.

'There's something else, isn't there?' Hagan asks.

'It seems young Ian was acting oddly. He'd also hurt his hand. That could explain the blood we found in the lift.

The Shaws were very disturbed by his behaviour. There's one other thing.'

Hagan waits without interrupting.

'The Shaws live on the same street as the old guy who phoned in about a possible abduction attempt.'

Hagan scratches the greying hair at his temple.

'If Chubby Barr's outfit has got Ian,' he says, 'we haven't got long to find him.'

'What will they do to Moore if they get him?' Lomas asks.

Hagan meets Lomas's eyes. 'What do you think?'

In the red Megane Ian has come to the same conclusion.

I've got to get away.

But McCullough has got his wrist in a firm grip and has Ian twisted round sideways with his arm pushed up his back. The boy is skewered on a bolt of pain that begins in the small of his back and stabs up through the base of his skull. The hand McCullough is gripping is the one Ian trapped in the lift doors. McCullough knows how to sustain pain so that it disables his opponent.

'You're hurting me,' Ian complains.

'Write to your MP about it,' McCullough retorts with cold humour. 'Billy here tells me you're a slippery wee customer. I'm not letting go of you, Ian boy, not until we've given your old da a ring and got him down here.'

Ian tries to struggle but McCullough simply applies more pressure. A sliver of agony slices through his upper arm and shoulder, finally crashing into the back of his head. He can hardly think, never mind escape.

'I wouldn't do that,' McCullough says. 'The more you fight it, the more it hurts. You're not doing yourself any favours.'

Ian tries once more before admitting defeat.

'There's got to be more we can do,' says Lomas.

'We're doing all we can,' says Hagan. 'You've got officers watching Rochester Avenue, haven't you?'

Lomas nods.

'We've applied for a search warrant. We'll be taking a look round the moment we get it.'

'And you've got men keeping an eye on the Shaws' house?'

Another nod.

'Not that I can see the boy coming back,' Lomas says, head sagging.

'Then all we can do is sit tight and wait for a break,' Hagan tells him.

He pats Lomas on the shoulder.

'And, believe me, we're long overdue one of them.'

The car is slowing down.

'Where are you taking me?' Ian asks.

McClean glances at him in the rear-view mirror.

'Somewhere we can all wait in comfort for Kenny.'

'He won't come,' Ian cries. 'He'll want to hear my voice. You're on to a loser there. There's no way you can make me say anything.'

In response, McCullough forces Ian's arm up between his shoulder blades. The pain corkscrews through his body and slams into the back of his eyes, forcing tears down his face. Ian cries out in agony.

'There you go,' says McClean, a note of satisfaction in his voice. 'That's all Kenny boy needs to hear and he'll come running.'

He stops the car and looks round.

'And Hughie here is an expert at causing pain.'

'You can have the money,' Ian says, forcing the words

out. 'Dad's hardly touched a penny of it. Just don't hurt him.'

'Get out of the car,' says McCullough, not interested in what Ian has to say. 'See the house with the satellite dish?'

Ian nods. 'The boarded-up one?'

'That's it. We're walking straight down the path and round the back. Try to struggle or call out and I'll break your arm. Do you understand?'

'Yes.'

'Good.'

He glances at McClean who has got out of the car and is looking up and down the street. McClean pulls out his mobile phone and makes a call.

'Chubby, it's me. We've got the boy. Yes, we're at the house. Five minutes then.'

Five minutes, thinks Ian. Five minutes and I'll be shut up in that house with the three of them. Five minutes and they'll have phoned Dad. Then it's all over. I've got to do something. But what?

McClean nods to give the all clear, then stops.

'What's that, Chubby? You found the address, did you? Clanton Drive?'

There was some other stuff, about a notebook in the van. Ian made a mental note of the address though. It might be important. Clanton Drive, he thinks. I know that. It's up by the retail park.

So what's in Clanton Drive?

'I know,' McClean is saying, still on the phone to Barr. 'Typical, isn't it? Still, finding the boy has saved us a lot of work. I know, tracking the house down was hardly worth the effort. We don't need it now we've got the boy.'

McCullough doesn't wait for McClean to finish on the phone. He shoves Ian forward, making him wince. That stupid steel comb, digging into the small of his back! Then a wave of heat spreads across his skin.

The comb!

Ian is half out of the car. McCullough is rocking forward to follow him. McClean is still talking to Chubby Barr on the mobile, watching a couple of kids kicking a ball about.

You won't get a better chance.

McCullough has Ian's right hand so it's got to be the left. He twists, shifts his weight, feels for the comb. His fingers close round the handle then work down until he is holding the comb by the teeth. Too late McCullough sees what he's doing.

'No!'

In the same instant Ian raises the comb and stabs down with all his strength, handle first, driving the point into the flesh of McCullough's thigh. He feels resistance, then sees the comb quivering in McCullough's leg and recoils. He feels like gagging. The shriek that explodes from McCullough's throat surprises Ian but the skull-headed man has relaxed his grip and that is all Ian needs. Stamping down on McCullough's foot and breaking free, he throws himself out of the vehicle and sets off down the road in a lurching run. Taken unawares, McClean makes a grab for him and cannons into McCullough as he follows Ian painfully out of the car. Ian hears them cursing but he isn't about to look back.

For the third time that day he is running for his life.

Seventeen

For three months after their meeting at Lou's wedding Kenny Kincaid and Tina Rea were inseparable. Kenny would finish work, have a wash and rush to her house. There he would sit in the Reas' cheerily decorated parlour and marvel at the suburban quiet. To his surprise, he was glad to leave the Shankill behind. Where Tina was living now you could almost believe you were in the Home Counties or some such place, far from Ulster's troubles and the demands of the Defenders. For the first time in his life, he started to realise that you could live without even caring what community, or what religion, you belonged to.

It wasn't long before Kenny and Tina were planning their future together. Everybody commented on the change in Kenny. His wild days seemed to be behind him. But not everybody was happy for him, as he discovered one summer's evening.

He and Tina were walking back to Kenny's house eating fish and chips when Chubby Barr and Billy McClean stepped out in front of them.

'Long time, no see, Kenny boy,' said Chubby.

'I've been busy,' said Kenny.

'Too busy to see your old mates?' Chubby asked. 'Is that what you mean, Kenny? Because if it is . . .'

'What's this in aid of, Chubby?' he asked.

'We've a job for you,' said Chubby.

Kenny glanced at Tina. She was frowning.

'What sort of a job?'

'Not here,' said Chubby. 'Meet us at Sam Mitchell's bar.'

When Chubby and Billy had gone, Tina wanted to know what that was all about. Her normally soft voice sounded tinny and anxious.

'Nothing,' said Kenny.

'You'll have to do better than that,' Tina told him. 'If we are to have a life together, there can be no secrets.'

Kenny nodded.

'No secrets, Tina. These are my friends. I can't just cut them off.'

'I've nothing against you having friends,' said Tina, placing a heavy, sceptical accent on that last word, 'but this . . .'

She curled a lock of hair behind her ear.

'They were talking about a job, Kenny. I'm not stupid and you're no angel.'

When he went to protest she placed a finger to his lips to block his words.

'These friends of yours come with a price tag attached.'

Kenny took her hands.

'Nothing will ever come between us,' he said. 'Trust me.'

'You can spare a minute for us then?' said Chubby, as Kenny crossed the floor of the smoky bar.

'What's all this about?' Kenny asked, taking a seat at the table.

'We need a third man,' said Chubby.

'What for?'

In answer Chubby laid a photograph face down on the table.

'Do you know who this is?'

Kenny turned the photo over. He recognised Joe McCann. The youth who had taunted them all those years ago was now a leading IRA man.

'You know I do.'

'He'll be at this address tomorrow night.'

Chubby pushed a piece of paper across the table.

'What's this got to do with me?'

'You swore the same oath as me and Billy,' Chubby said. 'To obey orders without question. We've had our orders. Battalion thinks we're ready. You're with the big boys now.'

'Look, I've never said no before, but this . . . I'm not sure, Chubby.'

Chubby laughed.

'The oath was for keeps,' he said.

Kenny found the steel he needed to stand up to Chubby.

'Nothing's for keeps,' he replied. 'Boots and fists is one thing. I can't do this.'

'Think again, Kenny boy,' said Chubby. 'This is what you used to dream about. We're big boys now. Time to come out to play.'

'Yes?' said Kenny, suddenly defiant. 'Well, I'm not playing.'

Chubby placed a hand on Kenny's arm, preventing him from standing.

'You took the oath, Kenny,' Chubby said.

Shrugging Chubby's hand away, Kenny got to his feet and turned to go. He was doing this for Tina.

'An oath is for life,' Chubby reminded him. 'Nobody walks away.'

Eighteen

Ian hurdles a crumbling brick wall and cuts down an alley. He finds himself in open ground facing three monstrous grey tower blocks standing in a row under the dark, stormy sky. Now he knows where he is – in the toughest part of town, an estate so deprived it is known to the locals as 'The Prison on the Hill', or simply The Prison. Once you take a hard-to-let round here, you're not going to leave in a hurry.

Sensing McClean behind him, Ian stumbles over the rubble. The rain is on and off, tears in the wind, and it has turned the brick dust slimy and treacherous underfoot. The heaped masonry and brickwork is all that can be seen of the first stage of the council's 'urban renewal' – the demolition of a row of vandalised maisonettes. Ian thinks about trying to phone Dad but he snatches a glance back at McClean. The wolfman is still following.

No time.

Sprinting across the waste ground, Ian can hear McClean behind him. For a man in his late thirties he certainly can shift. Ian had spent the entire car journey weighing up his captors. Both are lean and powerfully built, but McClean is the real hard man of the two. If anything, McClean is closing the gap on Ian.

There is no cover anywhere. Beyond the row of tower blocks there is more open space. The streets of vandalised terraced housing have been bulldozed, leaving a vast, aching openness. The way things are going, McClean has the beating of Ian over distance. He will overhaul him in a matter of seconds. Besides, thinks Ian, if I stay out in the open much longer McCullough will have got over the shock of being stabbed with the comb.

Ian spots somebody tapping his security code into the keypad by the front door of the nearest tower block. On impulse he listens for the click of the lock then springs forward. Forcing his body through the closing door, he follows the startled man inside.

'Calling on my gran,' he says. 'I'm the only company she gets.'

Though obviously suspicious the man makes no attempt to challenge Ian. The message in his eyes is unmistakable: *somebody else's problem.* Glancing back through a scratched and defaced glass panel, Ian sees McClean hammering on the door and glances at the man who has just let him in.

'Some people!' he says, before jogging up the stairs.

Pausing on the second landing, Ian is unsure what to do next. Should I phone the police, he thinks. Hell, Dad would probably kill me. Ian is shaking, almost paralysed with fear. His fingertips brush the phone, then slowly, agonisingly, he lets them drift away. No, it's your decision, Dad. I just hope you make the right one. If he had any plan at all when he tricked his way in, it was to hide in one of the many derelict flats in the block until McClean gave up. It isn't much of a plan, but it's the only one he's got.

He is on the fifth floor when he hears heavy footfalls on the stairs. He peers down the stairwell.

McClean?

Ian knows that if he can wangle his way inside so can McClean. Now he is looking in earnest. He runs up two flights before discovering the first empty flat. He decides to give it a miss. Too obvious. If he has got past the front door, McClean will probably check it out right away. Missing out two other empty flats on the eighth floor and the ninth, Ian tugs back the board covering the door of one on the eleventh. He's in luck. Behind the tacked-on hardboard the door is standing ajar. Ian tests the lock. It's still working. He lets himself inside and closes the door behind him. He presses the snib down to keep it locked.

Ugh! The place stinks!

What comes to Ian's nostrils is the smell of poverty and neglect: one part damp, two parts urine and two parts despair. There is a stained sleeping bag in one corner. It would be just my luck to find somebody in here, Ian thinks with a shudder. But there is nobody else. He explores the whole flat – both bedrooms, living room, bathroom, kitchen. It is completely empty. Making his way to the window, Ian looks out. He sees a red car pulling up outside the flats. It has to be McCullough. The noose is tightening. OK, Ian says, get a grip of yourself. Just sit tight.

Then what?

You've done it again, just like at the shopping centre – you've got yourself cornered. Skullhead is outside, standing guard, and by now the wolfman is probably inside the building, looking for you.

Ian's breath shudders in his chest. If there had been any other choice this would have been a stupid thing to do. But there wasn't. He chose the flats because there was nowhere else to go, no hiding place. He pulls out his mobile and thinks about Dad.

Nowhere else to go. That about sums it up. He doesn't

feel any better about the old man. For his secrets, for his past, Ian still hates him.

You let me down, Dad.

But I can't betray you.

Still not sure he is doing the right thing, Ian switches his phone on and makes the call.

'Dad? It's me.'

Quickly, he cuts the old man off.

'No, no questions,' he says. 'Just listen. I saw the cutting. I know about Mum.'

He hears Dad's shocked gasp and takes advantage of the silence that follows.

'Look,' he says. 'You know the three tower blocks on the Prison? Yes, that's right, up Cold Lane. Well, I'm in the one nearest the motorway. Of course I don't know the name of it! I told you, it's the one nearest the motorway – that shouldn't be hard to find. Yes, I'm in a flat on the eleventh floor. No, I'm not hurt. But listen, one of the men is probably inside by now, looking for me. McClean, I think he's called.'

He listens to the description Dad gives.

'Yes, that sounds like him. There's another man outside in the car.'

Dad asks a question.

'His name? I'm pretty sure it was Hugh. Yes, head like a skull, that's the one. Chubby? I think he'll be on his way by now. McClean called him before I got away.'

There are more questions.

'Dad, this isn't the time. I'll explain later. Just call the police.'

Ian ends the call and looks around. Have I done the right thing? he wonders. Now that Dad knows he's here, nothing will keep him from coming. Most likely he isn't going to phone the police either. Ian is still wondering whether to call Dad back when he hears a loud crash. It is coming from one of the lower floors. McClean! It's got to be. He's started kicking his way into the derelict flats and going through them room by room. He will work his way up, searching each systematically until he finds the right one.

'Now what?'

Ian runs to the window and peers down at the ground below. The red Megane is still there. Even while he's watching the green Rover joins it. Ian can see two men looking up at the flats. It has to be them: Chubby Barr and Hugh McCullough. Ian is still racking his brains when he hears footsteps outside on the landing. Moments later there is a noise like a thunderclap.

The wolf is at the door.

Nineteen

All through the engagement party Kenny Kincaid found himself looking round, searching for Chubby Barr. To his surprise, every time he located him in the crowd Chubby merely raised his glass in salute. Chubby seemed relaxed. All he wanted to do was enjoy himself. There was no mention of 'the orders'.

About ten o'clock Tina grabbed Kenny's hand and led him on to the dance floor.

'So what are you so edgy about?' she asked, reaching up to put her arms round his neck. 'Not having second thoughts, are you?'

'Who's edgy?' Kenny asked, his eyes flicking away from Tina's smiling face.

'You are. Does this have anything to do with Chubby?'

For the second time his gaze slipped away and roved the room.

'Don't be daft,' he snorted, a little too hurriedly. 'I told you, that's sorted.'

'Sorted, is it? I didn't know the Defenders were so easily put off. Seems I've heard it said that their oath is for life.'

Tina searched Kenny's face.

'Honest to God, Kenny, why did you have to take that

stupid oath? You're not fighting for God and Ulster. This isn't fighting the IRA, it's acting just like them.'

Kenny doesn't need telling. He has rubbed shoulders with men who revel in violence, Chubby and Billy among them. He used to hear tunes of glory on the Twelfth of July parades. Now it's the drumbeat of war.

'I was a kid, Tina, just a kid.'

Tina laid her head against his chest.

'I know, Kenny,' she breathed, 'but hatred's poisoning this place.'

Kenny leaned forward so that he could smell her perfume. He wanted to cling to the sway of her body, fall away into the dreamland of the music and her scent, but the oath was like a maggot, nibbling its way through the moment, calling him back to blood and tradition.

'We all make mistakes,' he said, his voice thick with emotion.

'You're right, Kenny,' she said. 'What worries me: anywhere else but here you get a chance to put them right. In this city second chances are hard to come by.'

Kenny cleared his throat. He loved this girl so much he could drown in her presence.

'Tina . . .'

'No, Kenny,' she said. 'Do anything you have to to put it right. Do it now, before you get in any deeper. Please, do it for me.'

Kenny nodded and drew away. Without a word, he crossed the floor looking for Chubby. On his way through the bar he walked into his da.

'Good to see you settling down,' Da said.

He was tottering. He'd had a glass too many. Kenny just hoped Tina's teetotal father couldn't see him.

'There was a time,' Da continued, 'you really had me worried.'

Kenny gave his father a watery smile.

'Ah, let the boy be!' Ma said.

But she had some words of her own.

'I'm really proud of you, Kenny,' she said. 'Tina's a lovely girl.'

Kenny squeezed Ma's arm.

'I know,' he said. 'I'm a lucky man.'

Having finally run the gauntlet of congratulations, Kenny went to find Chubby.

He came across him outside in the street.

'I've been waiting for you, Kenny boy,' Chubby said.

'You knew I'd come then?'

Chubby chuckled.

'What do you take me for, Kenny? Of course I knew you'd come. You're not the first man that's tried to pull out.'

'No,' said Kenny. 'But I'm the first that's meant it. There's nothing you can do to make me change my mind. I want the Defenders to cut me loose. I'm making a life for myself.'

Chubby snorted.

'Just because you've got a bit of skirt? Grow up, Kenny. There's a war going on, that's the whole North and South of it. Till it's won, nothing else matters. Remember what they did to Sam Mitchell's bar? Sam rebuilt it. You can put the bricks and mortar back together. What about people, Kenny? We're the men that stand between this community and the bombers. I'll ask you again: do you remember?'

Kenny wanted to clap his hands to his ears. You can shut out sounds, not memories. He remembered the concussive impact of the bomb.

'Of course I do, and the things our side has done to them. Remember the man the Battalion got for the bombing? They left him dead on wasteland. It turned out he didn't have anything to do with it. His crime was to be a Catholic

walking down the wrong street late at night. We're none of us so perfect, Chubby.'

'You're sounding just like a Fenian yourself, Kenny,' said Chubby.

'Don't be stupid,' Kenny snapped. 'No, I'm sounding like a man who's had enough.'

Kenny waited for Chubby to continue with the exchange. He didn't.

'I'll be seeing you then, Kenny,' Chubby said, setting off down the road where Billy McClean was waiting for him.

'You haven't told me,' Kenny said. 'Do you accept my resignation? Is it over?'

'Are those stars going to fall out of the sky?' Chubby asked. 'Kenny, what's it like in that dream world of yours?'

He spun on his heel and went into the night.

'It's never over.'

Twenty

Ian stares at the door. He sees the frame bow and bend under the impact of McClean's kick. One, maybe two, more good kicks and the door will burst open. Ian flies to the window. Below he can see Barr and McCullough. They don't see him.

Think, Ian. Think!

His feet take him to the kitchen. The window here looks out on to the side of the building where they can't see him.

What the hell am I doing?

He looks down, holding a conversation with this mad person who is directing his movements. There's a ledge. It's narrow, hopelessly fragile, but it might just support his weight.

Go out there? It's crazy.

But the wolf is at the door. Ian reaches out a trembling hand, then stops. The kitchen window isn't locked but it only comes open so far. There's a fitting. It's designed to prevent the window opening fully – obviously a safety device to protect children. In his mind's eye he can see Chubby Barr's gun. He imagines it pointed at Dad's head. It would be crazy to climb outside all right.

But if I let them take Dad I could be signing his death warrant!

Ian looks around frantically. He's got to jemmy off this restraining device. He opens the kitchen cupboards one by one. They're bare. Then he sees it. On top of one of the fitted cupboards there's a screwdriver. He seizes on it gratefully and starts to work on the window.

Come on. Come on!

McClean drives his foot into the door again and curses. Serves you right, Ian thinks, a smile of satisfaction spreading across his face.

He works the restraining device again. This time something comes loose. Ian gouges the wooden frame. Paint flakes away. The wood beneath splinters and two sunken screws crunch out of the frame. He's done it. But getting the window open is the easy bit. What he's got in mind – the thing this lunatic in his head is urging him to do – is more than difficult. It's impossible.

Climb out there? Eleven floors up? I can't. I just can't.

Ian pushes the window right open and sticks his head outside. The wind hits him like a fist. Needles of icy rain sting his eyes. He wants to give up the whole idea, but McClean isn't giving up. Ian hoists himself on to the middle of the frame, which bites into his diaphragm. Very slowly, his heart kicking at the inside of his sternum until it hurts, he clambers out. He hangs precariously on the window, willing it to support his weight, then starts to slide his right foot down the rough, pitted outside wall of the block. Gingerly, tentatively he reaches for the eight-inch ledge he saw when he looked out. Taking a last gulp of air, and clinging to the window, he feels for the ledge and finds it. Now it doesn't seem just narrow – it's hardly there at all. He can only fit part of his foot on it. It will mean taking the whole of his weight on his toes and the balls of his feet.

Jeez!

He tests the ledge with his right foot, feeling for cracks or crumbling masonry.

Ridiculous.

Stupid.

Suicide.

He sees the next balcony along – his objective if he is to get away from McClean.

I can't!

That's when the front door bursts open. It's as if somebody has taken a sledgehammer to the very air itself, compacting it under the blow. There's nothing else for it. Still gripping the window frame, Ian lowers his left foot after the right. Now his whole weight is resting on the ledge. At least it hasn't given way. It seems firm. He slides his fingers along the wall. Parallel to the ledge, about shoulder-height, he has found a thin crevice cut into the brickwork. It runs right along the building. If he can dig his fingers into that shallow crack and shuffle along the ledge he might just make it to the balcony a few metres away.

'Is anyone in there?'

It's McClean.

'Ian?'

I've got to get away from the window.

But how? How do you force yourself to move out along an eight-inch ledge with nothing but an eleven-storey drop beneath your feet? Imagine, Ian tells himself, one slip, one false move and you will explode on the ground like a ripe tomato. How do you take that first, gut-wrenching step? But what is in the room is worse than what is waiting out here in the buffeting wind.

Move!

Ian can hear McClean prowling around inside. Taking another deep breath he makes the first step. Digging his fingers into the thin crevice like claws, he edges away from the window. His legs are shuddering like the gear-stick of a stationary vehicle.

Don't look down, he tells himself. Don't you dare look down!

Then there's a loud bang next to his ear. The wind has prised the window off its latch and made it slam. He very nearly falls at that moment. He can feel his body coming away from the wall, like a suction pad coming loose.

No! I won't fall. I refuse to die.

He forces his whole body against the wall. His clammy palms and his face are pressed against the mercilessly rough and pitted surface. Where he trapped his hand in the lift doors this morning, there is a gnawing ache that won't go away.

I refuse to die.

I refuse!

Out here in the whining, buffeting wind and the pattering rain the sounds from inside the flat are lost, muffled. But Ian can imagine McClean rushing to the kitchen, drawn by the sound of the window slamming. He forces himself against the window, hoping against hope that McClean isn't going to look out. Gradually he turns his head to see. His nose is pressed into the wall.

Nearly there now.

He succeeds in turning his head all the way round. He wishes he hadn't. McClean is at the window. A moment later he has stuck his head outside.

Twenty-One

It was over as far as Kenny was concerned. The fighting, the bigotry, the ancestral loyalties – he'd lived for them once. Now he had found something else to live for, something bigger than the hatreds that seeped like acid into the foundations of this city. He was living, quite simply, for love.

Ma couldn't believe her luck. There was Lou, Queen of Wimpeyland, settled into her suburban three-bedroomed semi with her peeler as Kenny insisted on calling him, or Andy as he was known to the rest of the family. Now Kenny had turned his back on his wild youth and was planning to follow in Lou's footsteps and marry in the spring.

The talk was that Chubby and Billy still wanted Kenny for the big job. They hadn't been idle though. A young man had been taken to a roadside and the flesh from above his kneecap shot away. He would walk again, maybe. Chubby and Billy had roped in a new recruit by the name of Hugh McCullough. Kenny had seen him around – a tall, lean, emotionless man. He was short on friends but big on violence. Kenny didn't like the look of McCullough at all. He was the kind of man who got a buzz from all this: the beatings, the punishment shootings, walking round his home streets playing the big man.

'What are you thinking about?' Tina asked, reaching round and curling her slender fingers round his neck.

'I was just thinking about Lou,' he replied, not entirely truthfully. 'She's got everything – the house, the garden, the car. Honest to God. I'd get you the world if I could. I just wish I could run to a house like hers.'

'We'll get there eventually,' said Tina.

'Aye,' said Kenny. 'Of course we will.' But he knew ever since Lou had told them she was expecting her first baby that that was what Tina wanted too – a child of their own.

The following Sunday Kenny was going fishing with Da. Kenny was about to shut the boot of the car when Da told him to wait up a minute.

'I've left the flasks on the kitchen table.'

Kenny was standing by the open boot when Chubby and Billy arrived.

'Fishing is it, Kenny?'

'Cut the small talk,' Kenny said. 'What is it you want, Chubby?'

'I've got something for you.'

Chubby pulled a package from his jacket. He put it down in the boot, next to the rods. 'Want to take a look?'

'What is it?' Kenny asked, though he already knew.

Chubby unwrapped his gift. It was a revolver.

'You missed our last outing, Kenny,' said Chubby. 'We were wondering if you were ready to come out to play. McCann's still strutting round like he owns half of west Belfast.'

Kenny hurriedly wrapped the gun and handed it back to Chubby. At that moment Da came out of the house with the flasks and watched Chubby and Billy walking off down the street.

'What did those two want?' he asked suspiciously.

Kenny shrugged. 'Does it matter? Come on, Da. Let's go catch some fish.'

Twenty-Two

Ian is clinging to the wall, his face pressed into it, the muscles in his leg starting to buzz and ache, the tendons round his ankles tugging as they take the strain of holding him on that eight-inch ledge. But that is only half of it. McClean's head is sticking out of the window no more than a yard or two away.

Have you seen me? You must have.

But McClean is squinting straight ahead. He squeezes the rain from his eyes. He's half-blinded by the whip and sting of the wind.

What the hell is this? You must have seen me.

Ian almost wants to be seen. Then it will be over. No troughs of despair, no peaks of hope, just the acceptance of your fate.

Closure.

But McClean's eyes fail to fasten on Ian. The wolfman looks down not sideways, then, incredibly, he starts to withdraw his head. A moment later Ian hears the click of the catch. There is no way back. He has to go forward. Even as he braces himself to take his first step he can't believe he hasn't been seen.

This is just a stupid game of cat and mouse. It's got to be.

How can you have missed me? You must have seen me. You must!

But as quickly as he appeared McClean has gone. It's too good to be true. Ian tries to imagine himself in McClean's place. Could I possibly be that close to somebody and not see anything?

No, you've seen me.

I know what this is. You're just going to work your way round to the other side of the building and wait for me there.

Cold as it is up there on his precarious eleventh-floor perch, Ian is sweating. His palms are slimy against the wall. Ever so slowly he moves his right hand from the wall and wipes it on his shirt. Then, returning his right hand to the wall and easing his left off, he repeats the operation. Finally, realising he has no choice but to go on, he makes his first move since McClean's head appeared at the window.

Trying not to look down the dizzying precipice of the building, Ian takes the weight on his toes and on the balls of his feet and starts to inch forward. A few more steps and those aching muscles will be shrieking with pain.

You can do this, he tells himself.

He barks insults at himself under his breath. Coward! Idiot! It doesn't matter how much noise he makes, not in this howling wind.

Come on! You can do it.

But, as he feels the tendons in his legs starting to shudder again, as he feels the wind trying to suck him off the wall, he isn't sure he can.

Peter Moore is back in the blue VW. No matter how exposed he is in the car, he is worse off without it. He has parked in a side street to the left of the row of tower blocks.

A vandalised bus stop, the old style made of pebble-dashed concrete, shields him from view. From his vantage point he can see everything. He can see the blocks – three grey, hope-starved sisters drawn up in battle formation on the edge of night. He can see Chubby Barr and Hugh McCullough standing by their cars. The only thing he can't see is his fourteen-year-old son inching along an eight-inch ledge. He knows nothing of the drama unfolding round the corner of the nearest tower block.

'So where are you now, Ian?' he wonders out loud.

The best bet is in one of those flats. Most likely Ian is still holed up on the eleventh floor, the place he phoned from. Moore looks across at Barr and McCullough. They'll be armed, the pair of them. Same goes for McClean, wherever he is.

So no way I can just go in blazing. No, you'll have to come to me, Ian.

Moore takes his mobile from his pocket.

The mobile shrills in Ian's pocket. Panic rushes through him, a wave of heat as if from a duct below his feet. But there is nothing beneath Ian's feet – just a sickening fall to the ground. His heels are out over the drop, trembling precariously. One false move and he is gone. Ian listens to the ring tone and he wants to cry.

What possessed me to choose the Simpsons theme tune?

Insanely, Ian can see it all imprinted on his mind: Lisa on her bike, Bart on his skateboard, Marge and Maggie in the car and, finally, Homer being chased through the garage.

And me up this tower block.

D'oh!

D'oh!

Double D'oh!

Sliding his right hand down the wall, biting his lip

against the crackle of pain that fizzes through his palm, Ian starts to paw at his trousers, feeling for the mobile. Then, before he can get his hand in his pocket, the tone stops. Ian feels his body slacken against the brickwork but immediately forces it taut again.

No, no relaxing.

Keep concentrating.

He knows that the keenness of his mind is all that is standing between him and fatal impact with the ground below. So, heels over the drop, toes clinging to the ledge, he edges forward, sliding his feet. And it is left foot, right foot, palms flattened against the bricks, fingernails clawing at the shallow crevice.

Not far now.

He continues to shuffle along the ledge. His movements are slow and deliberate, all the more so because of the rain that is trickling down the brickwork, sluicing over the ledge and puddling round his feet.

A few more steps.

On he goes. Out of the corner of his eye he can see street lamps and the necklace of lights strung out along the motorway. The night wind is a dark muzzle sucking at him, nibbling and gnawing at him, trying to chew him loose off that wall.

Just a few more steps.

There's the balcony! With a little stretching he could put his hand on the rail.

But I mustn't. If I rush now I could throw it all away.

Instead, Ian actually forces himself, completely against instinct, to slow down. Legs quivering, muscles crying out, he shuffles slowly along to the balcony. Then he can't move any more. He tries to take a step, but something is holding his foot to the ledge.

This can't be happening.

He tries to see what can be glueing him to the ledge like this. His whole body quivering, the rain dripping off his eyebrows and his nose, he slides his forehead down the brickwork. There's the ground below.

Oh God. Oh my God!

D'oh, d'oh and double d'oh!

He tries to shift his foot, doing it by force, kicking at the obstruction. It's the wrong move. The sole of his shoe slips off the ledge. Slithers into the black void below him. Death has hold of his ankle, pulling him down.

No!

He wants to scream but he bites down the terror and clamps his foot back on the ledge. He gulps down icy breaths of air.

Oh Jeez!

Now he can see. His right shoelace has come undone and he is standing on it with his left. Even after kicking his foot right off the ledge he has stood back down on it.

Stupid!

He raises his foot and shakes the wet shoelace from the sole of his shoe. He does it carefully this time. With control. He is free. Wearily, hardly able to believe that it is over, he hauls himself over the balcony rail then slides down and lies exhausted on the other side.

Moore stares at his mobile.

Now what?

Maybe Ian is unable to answer. Maybe he daren't. What if the ring tone is going to give away his hiding place?

Moore takes a long, deep breath, as if trying to suck every ounce of strength and knowledge and ingenuity from deep down inside himself. He sees Tina's dark eyes looking at him full of love and pleading.

This is our son I'm trying to save, he tells her. But how? How do I do it?

But Kenny Kincaid didn't believe in miracles when the car bomb ripped his wife apart and neither does Peter Moore.

Tina can't speak from beyond the grave.

There is nobody to help him.

He is quite alone.

Ian picks himself up and looks around. The first thing he notices is the flickering glow of a TV screen. He is on the balcony of an occupied flat. For a moment or two he even considers climbing out again but one look at the eight-inch ledge and Death waiting in the howling darkness and he knows he could never do that again.

The balcony doors are covered by long net curtains. Ian crawls forward on his elbows and peers through them. He can only see one occupant – a fragile old lady seventy, maybe eighty years old. What's she doing living eleven floors up a tower block? Aren't the old folk supposed to get bungalows these days?

Ian sits up and leans his back against the wall. He blots his palms against his clothes. He is in two minds. Does he walk through the flat like it's the most natural thing in the world? Or does he stay put and wait his chance? He has more or less opted for the second alternative when the decision is taken out of his hands.

His phone rings.

'Ian?'

'It's me.'

'What's up?' Moore asks. 'Can't you talk?'

'I would have thought that was obvious. Listen, Dad,

I'm on the balcony of one of the flats. There's somebody inside. What? No, they don't know I'm here.'

But Ian is wrong. At that very moment the balcony doors swing open. He finds himself looking up at the pensioner.

'Who are you?' she croaks.

She looks frightened. Ian scrambles to his feet and she backs off.

'No,' he says. 'Don't be scared. I'm not trying to rob you or anything.'

Distrust hangs in her eyes.

'What are you doing on my balcony?' she asks.

Her voice is trembling. Her chin wobbles as she speaks again.

'How did you get out there?'

'It's a long story.'

Ian's eyes are pleading with her, begging her not to scream. Somewhere there is a wolf and he is still at the door.

'Listen,' Ian says, 'I don't mean you any harm. Just step back and I'll leave. I want to get out of here, that's all. That's it. I'm walking right out of here.'

Ian raises his hands. It's his way of showing the old girl he means what he says. It doesn't do much good. The moment he takes his first step forward, he sees her flinch.

'Honest, I'm not going to do anything. I just want to get out of here. I'm just as scared as you are. Please, don't try to call for help.'

Ian sees her eyes change. What did I say that for? I've actually put it in her mind. She hadn't even thought of it till now.

Oh, way to go, dumb cluck.

'Look,' he says, 'I'm going to the door. See? This is me leaving.'

As Ian moves in a wide semi-circle round the old lady he is aware of Dad still talking on the phone. The confused, disembodied words crackle round him.

'Ian, Ian! What's going on?'

But there is no time to answer. Ian continues to edge towards the door, feeling for the door handle.

'Please don't scream,' he says. 'I know there's no reason to trust me, but I'm not a thief. I just want to get out of here.'

He is standing with his back to the door. The old lady actually seems to be giving him the benefit of the doubt!

Reaching behind, Ian finally curls his fingers round the door handle and lets himself out on to the landing. No sooner is he through the door than she starts screaming the place down. As he flees down the stairwell her shrieks are echoing off the walls, demons of sound in flight.

So much for benefit of the doubt!

Twenty-Three

It was an effort but, after three uneventful weeks, Kenny finally managed to put Chubby to the back of his mind. He had better things to think about. There was the church, the reception, the cars. Tina had taken charge of the rest: what they were going to wear, the colour of the bridesmaids' outfits, the honeymoon arrangements, that sort of thing. Either way, Kenny still felt he had a lot on his mind, and it just about squeezed Chubby out of his thoughts.

Kenny was working when it happened, the thing that changed his life for good. Not that he knew anything of the events until later. He went straight from work to a hotel close to Tina's. He did it on impulse. They had chosen to hold the reception somewhere up there, away from the Shankill. If Tina had had her way, they would have moved out of the city entirely and left Belfast and all its memories behind them. She still had all the stuff for Canada. But Ma and Da had begged them to stay. Kenny didn't have anything to do with the Defenders any more, so why leave?

Nobody knew he was at the hotel, not even Tina. He wasn't keeping it a secret. It was just that a workmate had suggested a little out-of-the-way place his brother had found. Kenny and Tina hadn't been happy with the original venue and this hotel sounded perfect. He wanted to get up there before he lost the booking. For nearly an hour Kenny discussed the buffet, seating arrangements and a dozen other things, any one of which would usually have had him running for the nearest bar. This time he stayed put, however. He was doing it for Tina.

It was close to noon when he paid the taxi driver and popped into a bar for a pint. It wasn't Sam Mitchell's he chose, of course. He wanted to stay out of Chubby's way. He thought about phoning Tina, but she would be busy with the bridesmaids' dresses. They were giving Tina and her ma a lot of headaches.

Kenny finally left the bar about half past one and walked smack bang into Chubby on the street corner. The expression on Chubby's face took him by surprise. Gone was his usual air of controlled menace. He looked . . . shocked.

'I didn't expect to find you here,' Chubby said.

For once it was Chubby who seemed reluctant to talk.

'What do you mean?' Kenny asked.

Chubby searched Kenny's face for a moment, then gasped.

'Dear God, you don't know, do you?'

Kenny's bones froze to the marrow.

'Chubby, what are you telling me?'

'It's Lou's peeler, Kenny. He's been whacked. The Provies done him.'

Something snapped through Kenny's brain, a silent, mental scream.

'What about Lou? What about the baby?'

Chubby shook his head.

'The husband's the only one dead. That's all I know, Kenny.'

Kenny's legs melted inside. He stood still for a moment,

almost reeling back on his heels, then he ran. He was home in a couple of minutes. The first person he saw was Da. He looked at Kenny with eyes that were half-dead, focusing on something far away.

'In there, Kenny,' he said finally.

Kenny walked into the living room and saw Ma and Lou on the sofa, huddled together, very still, not crying at all.

'I just heard,' he said. 'I went to the hotel . . . met Chubby . . . Is he . . . ?'

Ma took Lou's head in her hands as if trying to drown out the sounds of the world. She drew Lou to her then looked at Kenny and nodded. Lou's peeler . . . Andy . . . was dead.

'Lou, I'm . . .'

The words stalled in his throat and for a long while he couldn't speak at all. Then he managed something – not enough, but something.

'So sorry, Lou. So very sorry.'

The words were no sooner out of his mouth than a shriek ripped through Lou. Her whole body shuddered.

'What is it, darling?' cried Ma, trying to hold Lou still while the new horror crashed over her.

'It's blood,' said Lou in a choking voice. 'It's blood.'

Two hours later they heard that Lou's baby was dead, miscarried. A nurse came along first and told them she didn't know anything. The doctor was next. He gave them the news they'd been dreading. Ma collapsed into a plastic chair and sobbed uncontrollably. As for Da, he was a dead soul. He just stood quietly further up the corridor, slowly breaking apart. His rheumy, half-dead eyes stared at nothing in particular and he mouthed a silent question.

Why?

Kenny did none of those things. He wasn't sorry any more. He wasn't distraught or reduced to tears. He wasn't

133

bewildered. Suddenly he was filled with a rage as desolate as the baby's loss. It was complete, hard and impenetrable as a diamond, and it filled him. There was no room for Tina or the wedding. There was no room for hope. All there was was vengeance. The first chance he had, he made his excuses and left.

He had something to do.

He met the boys in the room behind Sam Mitchell's cellar.

There were five men present, including Kenny. Chubby, Billy and Hugh were there. The fourth man was their officer commanding. It was much like Kenny's first visit to the room, the day he was sworn in as a Young Defender. Kenny let the memories swim up for a moment then stepped forward to take the second oath of his life. Just like last time, a Union flag was spread across a table and on it lay a Bible. This time, however, there was something else.

Next to the Bible lay a loaded revolver.

Twenty-Four

One thing Ian knows for certain – the wolfman is coming. Somewhere, in one of the flats or on one of the landings, Billy McClean has heard the old woman's scream. Right now, at this very moment, from wherever he went after smashing his way into the eleventh-floor flat and finding nobody there, he is climbing or descending the stairs, heading for the source of that scream. Ian is bounding down the stairs two at a time, panting, gulping in air in fevered snatches.

What now?

He stops, leaning back against a wall. It is as if fear itself is cascading down the walls, the way the icy rain ran over him out there on the ledge. Then a faint crackle reminds him his phone is still on.

'Dad?'

'Why don't you answer your phone? What the hell is happening?'

'I'm being followed. I've got to get out.'

'Get to a balcony,' Moore tells him. 'Don't go down to the front door. They're watching it. It'll have to be the first-floor balcony, out of sight of the main door.'

'But those flats are all occupied,' Ian protests. 'I checked on the way up.'

'Don't argue, Ian. We've got this one chance. I don't care how you do it, but find a first-floor balcony and jump. I'll be there with the car.'

Ian nods though there is nobody to see him make the gesture. He switches off and bounds down two flights of stairs, counting the floors.

Six . . . five . . .

Somewhere in the flats he can hear an unseen but familiar presence making his way downstairs. The wolfman.

Go!

Three . . . or is it four?

Ian pounds downstairs. There are no numbers painted on the walls to indicate the floors so he hopes he's got it right. He jumps and lands heavily on the ground-floor landing. In front of him there are two doors, flats 7 and 7A. He hammers on number 7. Nothing. He can hear the heavy footfalls approaching from above. The wolfman. He runs to number 7A. Then, just when he has finished rapping on the door, number 7 opens and a kid, maybe eight years old, sticks her head out.

'Who are you?'

Ian doesn't answer. Why waste time? Instead he pushes past into the flat. The girl immediately starts bawling.

'Mum!'

Ian hears a plate smash in the kitchen but he isn't hanging round. He did enough explaining to the old woman.

'Mummy! Mummy!'

Great! First a pensioner, now a kid! Ian races for the balcony. The doors are locked, most likely a security measure to keep the kid inside. Hearing the woman talking to her daughter, Ian looks round desperately. The last thing he needs now is to become embroiled in some stupid dispute. His eyes fall on an iron and he swings it through the pane of glass in the door. At the sound of breaking glass, mother and daughter begin to shriek in panic.

No time to lose. Got to get out.

Tapping away the jagged splinters left in the door, Ian squeezes through, clambers on to the balcony rail, and jumps into the night. The next thing he knows there is grass in his mouth and the heavy scent of soil in his nostrils. He is lying face down on the ground. His ribs and his right arm ache.

I must have counted wrong. That was the first *floor.*

Ian scrambles to his feet and looks around. He registers two things: to his right the wolfman is preparing to jump. To his left the blue VW is bouncing across the waste ground. For some reason Dad is driving without head-lights.

'Dad!'

The VW's engine screams as it crashes over the uneven ground. Ian starts to run towards it. Behind him he hears the thud as the wolfman hits the ground. A cry of pain splits the night. He is on his knees and holding his wrist.

I hope it's broken.

The VW swerves and comes to a halt, rocking on its chassis.

'Get in!'

The door is open and Dad is leaning forward, waving Ian inside. Ian is simultaneously aware of the wolfman running towards him and two car engines springing to life.

'Get in! Now!'

Ian throws himself into the passenger seat. He is now aware of people standing on the balconies of the three tower blocks watching the chase. He sees them, dark figures silhouetted against the room lights behind them. As Dad swings the VW over towards the road, the green Rover and the red Megane come into sight round the corner of the building. The car is skidding, spitting up dirt. The tyres spin, clawing for purchase on the slimy earth, then they grip and the car shoots forward.

Twenty-Five

Kenny Kincaid sat in the car, watching the house.

'You're sure he's the one?'

The day Lou's baby died Kenny was ready to put half of West Belfast to the sword and the flame. Four days later, as he sat in the car, the gun lying heavy on his lap, his rage was being eaten away at the edges, doubt and uncertainty showing through. That was Kenny Kincaid's problem – he couldn't forget how to be human. Sitting in the hospital, seeing Ma crying and Da standing bewildered like that, Kenny had become a creature all made of revenge. But here, on a drizzly Belfast night, the part of him that was still human, not consumed by primal hatred, the part of him that wanted a life with Tina and kids of his own, was alive and speaking to him.

Think what you're doing, Kenny.

That's a man in that house, a man like you.

But he had seen what this man had done. He had seen the effects of putting your humanity to one side. Two lives snuffed out, another made barren and waste. Their target was Joe McCann. No, he's not a man like me, Kenny thought. He couldn't be. This is a terrorist, a man lower than the animals.

Kenny had seen the shattered look in Lou's eyes. He had heard the way her voice split open, the way she splintered and cracked inside, and that was all down to this Taig, this dirty terrorist. With her husband and child dead, Lou was an empty vessel. Her beauty withered away overnight, leaving a woman whose lungs filled and emptied, whose heart pumped, but who didn't live. Hope wasn't there any more. Kenny couldn't give her her family back but he could give her justice. He could give her a sense that somewhere in this empty world there were men who could put things right.

Soldiers.

'It's half past three,' said Chubby Barr. 'Time to go in.'

He gave Kenny a sidelong glance.

'Sure you're ready for this, Kenny?'

Kenny's voice came back, cold and hard like the revolver's metal.

'I'm ready.'

'Fair enough,' said Chubby. 'From now on, no names.'

He looked at each man in turn.

'Move fast, hit hard and leave. No talk. Is that clear?'

The men's silence was enough to tell Chubby they understood. He nodded twice, once in response to Kenny, once to set things in motion. Billy McClean stayed with the car, sliding down in the driver's seat, making himself at home in the darkness. Chubby took the sledgehammer from the boot. Hugh brought up the rear. After that everything seemed to happen in slow motion, like an old film stuttering through a sequence of stills. Later Kenny would remember his breath coming back on his face from the woollen balaclava, spittle forming on it and making it cold and uncomfortable on his cheeks and lips.

They were running round the back. Then there was the explosion as the sledgehammer did its job on the kitchen door. Metal crunched and wood splinters flew like tiny blowdarts. They were through the back door and pounding upstairs. A child whimpered. After that there was another freeze-frame. This time it was Kenny at the bedroom door, then moving across the room, dragging his man out of bed. In the days that followed Kenny's mind would shudder through the events, visiting the ghostly, strobed images of terror: the victim's face white, fear as tight as cling-film on his features; the wife sitting up screaming; voices ricocheting off the walls.

'Do it!'

Chubby's voice crackled across the room. His eyes fixed Kenny through the holes in his balaclava.

'Do him and we're gone!'

Kenny's finger was on the trigger but he didn't squeeze. He'd seen something – a ridiculous detail. This man, this killer, he had the same alarm clock as Kenny Kincaid. McCann was a husband, a father to his kids. All of a sudden it wasn't in Kenny to finish the man. He didn't see a Taig, he saw a human being.

You've got your truth, Kenny thought, your tricolour and your faith. I've got mine. And we're both ready to kill for them. Who says they aren't equal? For all that McCann had done to Lou and her peeler, he couldn't fire the gun. By now Chubby was bawling over the screaming of the wife.

'Do him!'

Kenny saw McCann scrambling under the bed. His fingers were scratching on the threads of the carpet, trying to retrieve something.

'He's going for his guns!'

The gun roared and Chubby screamed.

'I'm hit! For God's sake, finish him!'

Then another reality roared in Kenny's head. This was gun against gun, man against man. The man had killed Andy. He had killed Lou's baby. Now he had shot Chubby.

Kenny squeezed the trigger.

His mind was raked with sound.

The shot bounced McCann back against the wall. The lifeless body slumped to the floor like a sack.

Kenny had done it.

McCann was as dead as Andy, as dead as Lou's baby.

'Let's get out of here,' Hugh said.

But Kenny could only stand and watch as the thick, dark blood pillowed his victim's head. The wife's screams clawed at his mind. Funny thing that, how Taig pain sounded just like Prod pain.

'Kenny . . .'

Hurt as he was, Chubby yelled an order.

'No names. I said there were to be no names.'

Kenny saw the blood staining Chubby's right sleeve. He saw the Fenian's blood spreading across the carpet. The victim wasn't the only dead man in the room. The man Tina Rea loved was drowning in all that blood.

Twenty-Six

Dad floors the accelerator and bounces the car over banking that borders North Perimeter Road.

'Chubby chose the area well,' Dad says, fighting to bring the rocking, pitching vehicle under control.

His words are coming in snatches.

'This road is nearly deserted. We've got to get among some traffic.'

Dad looks across and his eyes flash.

'Get that belt on!' he barks, seeing Ian rolling round the front seat.

His face twisting, Ian does as he is told. His hand is still on the seatbelt buckle when he sees the Megane coming up in the passenger-side wing mirror.

'He's trying to take you on the inside!'

Dad swings the car over to the left. The Megane has to brake. It loses momentum and falls back. Ian sees the old man check his rear-view mirror. He's going to do something.

'Hold on,' Dad orders.

Ian is about to ask what he has in mind.

Dad silences him with a look, then snaps the car into a handbrake turn. Ian sees the look on Chubby's face as the

VW deals the green Rover a glancing blow. Dad lets the steering wheel spin through his hands for a moment then grips hard and takes off down the road. Ian twists round. The Rover has crashed into a lamp post and Chubby is running to join Billy and Hugh in the Megane.

'Where did you learn to do that?' Ian asks.

'Let's call it a misspent youth,' says Dad.

There is more than a hint of satisfaction in his voice.

Lomas puts down the phone and looks at Hagan.

'We've found Moore,' he says.

'Where?'

'North Perimeter Road. It looks like the gang's found him too. There are reports of a car chase.'

Hagan slaps a map down in front of Lomas.

'Show me,' Hagan says.

Lomas traces the road from The Prison flats towards town.

'How many vehicles?'

'Three. Moore and the boy are in one. The other two in pursuit.'

'If I know Kenny he'll be heading into heavy traffic to lose them.'

Suddenly Hagan isn't saying Moore.

'This is a dangerous situation,' says Lomas.

'Right,' says Hagan. 'Let's get up there.'

'No! Oh no!'

Ian sees Dad's problem. The lights are on red and both lanes of the carriageway are backed up.

'Come on,' says Dad, snatching a look in the rear-view mirror. 'Go green! Go green! Change, will you?'

He is slowing.

'Are they behind us?' Dad asks. 'I don't see them.'

Ian cranes to see.

'No. Hang on – yes, there they are, three cars back.'

McCullough has just opened the Megane's passenger door. He's coming after them on foot.

'Dad!'

'I know. I see him.'

That's when the lights change. The cars begin to move but not quickly enough for Dad. He starts pounding on the steering wheel.

'Come on!' he yells. 'Move, for crying out loud. Go. Go!'

But McCullough is alongside. He starts tugging at the door handle. It doesn't budge. Dad has locked it from the inside. McCullough is still pulling at the handle when Dad changes up into second, then third. The car's momentum spins the attacker half off his feet. McCullough is forced to let go.

'Oh, come on!' says Dad. 'Move!'

But before he can ease the VW out of the congestion there is a loud crunch of metal, throwing the pair of them forward. It's as if a fist has just slugged them from behind. McClean has accelerated hard and slammed another vehicle into the back of them. In turn, the VW slams into the car in front and the airbags detonate. The seat belts kick in and hold them rigid. But nothing can stop their heads snapping forward with the car's momentum, smacking off the air bags. Ian is still whipping back and forth when Dad's face rips through the confusion.

'Ian, are you all right?'

'What?'

The night is booming around him, the lights spinning as he tries to focus.

'Yes . . . I think so.'

Before Ian can finish speaking Dad is kicking at his door, trying to force it open.

'Jammed. What about your side?'

Ian tries the handle.

'Hang on, it's locked.'

He flips the catch.

'Now it's open.'

But just as Ian is shoving at it, McCullough comes skidding round the back of the car for a second go and makes a lunge for him. In the split-second that Ian shrinks back with fright he feels Dad pushing against his shoulder, reaching across him.

'What are you doing?'

Dad pulls something out of a rolled up carrier bag.

A gun.

'We've got armed officers on the way,' Lomas says.

'How long will that take?' Hagan asks.

'Ten, fifteen minutes.'

'Too late. We've got to go in ourselves.'

Lomas's head snaps round to look at Hagan.

'We don't even know what we're walking into.'

Hagan's eyes wrinkle with amusement.

'No, but we've got a pretty good idea.'

Dad shoves Ian out of the car and follows him on to the street. Ian staggers a little. He's still half in the spinning world of the collision. He is aware of the street lights on the rain-slicked streets, of cars slewed across the road, of McCullough backing off and a small crowd of people looking on. Faces tilt in the rain. Colours are smudged in the darkness. Meanwhile a heavily-built, balding man is examining the damage to his car. His is one of several vehicles damaged when the Megane rammed the car behind Dad. The man looks up and sees Barr and McClean approaching.

'Have you seen what you've done to my car?' he yells, going towards them. 'What kind of speed do you call that? I could have whiplash because of you.'

He feels in his pocket for a pen.

'I want your insurance details,' he says. 'Now.'

He is about to say something else when McClean cuffs him across the bonnet of the nearest car.

'Shut it, fat boy!'

The man slides to the floor, eyes shocked wide. Protests rise from the crowd. But nobody moves.

'There's something up ahead,' says Lomas.

The rain is steady, reducing visibility. Hagan strains to see what's happening.

'That has to be Kenny,' says Hagan. 'Who else is going to create this much mayhem?'

Lomas can't help feeling there is a touch of admiration in Hagan's words.

'I can't take the car any further,' he says, again wondering about Hagan's values. 'We'd better get out.'

The three men are walking forward when they hear a gunshot.

Dad can't see any alternative. With McCullough ahead of him and Barr and McClean coming up on his right he raises the gun and fires a shot. People in the small crowd start running and diving for cover. Barr and McClean are carried backwards by the press of running onlookers. Dad changes his grip on the revolver and whips McCullough across the face, opening a deep wound.

'Come on, Ian!'

Ian stares in disbelief. There is nothing for it but to run. He follows Dad down an alleyway. Even halfway down it, the sounds of the street are falling away already.

'Dad, this is crazy!'

Dad is shoving the gun in his belt.

'Don't talk, run!'

They reach the far end of the alley.

'Left.'

Ian wants to protest but Dad is so certain. Without him, Ian would have collapsed to the floor in despair minutes ago. But while he is there, obedience is the only way. They run and the night closes around them.

By the time Lomas and Hagan arrive by the concertinaed cars all the main players have gone. At the sight of the uniformed officers who have followed the plainclothes men to the scene, members of the public come running forward with their stories.

Hagan shoves his way through the crush. No Kenny. No Ian. No Barr, McClean or McCullough either.

'We've missed them,' he growls.

'We'll pick them up again,' says Lomas. 'Let's face it, they're not exactly shrinking violets.'

'We'd better,' says Hagan.

Lomas frowns.

'Meaning?'

'I thought I'd made the stakes clear,' says Hagan. 'This isn't just about the money. As far as Chubby's concerned, one of his own has turned.'

Hagan stares deep into Lomas's eyes.

'It's a blood feud.'

Twenty-Seven

Dad leads the way into the house. He stops in the hall and opens the below-stairs cupboard. Ian waits behind him, looking round the unfamiliar surroundings, while he punches in the alarm code then draws the curtains and switches on the lights. Ian notices that – the way Dad draws the curtains first, then goes over to the light switch. No point giving the enemy a free look at you.

'What's that smell?' Ian asks.

'Plaster,' Dad replies. 'Mr Ryan the owner wants all the walls skimming before he moves in.'

He gestures in the direction of the kitchen. Ian looks inside and sees the aluminium step ladder, the bags of plaster, the buckets and tools and, finally, the freshly-plastered walls. Three walls are almost dry. The other is a two-tone combination of light and dark brown. Dad was obviously in the middle of the job when his past exploded round him.

'You mean he trusts you with the keys?' Ian asks.

'It's no big deal,' says Dad. 'He hasn't moved anything in yet. Nothing to steal. If he wants to be sure, the day he moves in, all he has to do is change the locks and the alarm code. He isn't taking a risk having me in.'

He closes the door and looks at Ian.

'I suppose we should talk.'

'What we do next, you mean?' Ian asks. 'Don't worry, Dad, I'm resigned to clearing out. I know we can't stay.'

He is finding it hard to go on hating the old man. The first shock at discovering his mother was murdered has faded away, leaving emptiness and acceptance.

'I'll go with you,' Ian says. 'It's the only way.'

There's no mention of Vicky, though it will still hurt to let her go. So early in their relationship, Ian is sure they've got something special going.

'Oh, after what's happened I think that's already settled,' Dad says. 'There's no future for us in this town. We get our heads down here tonight. Tomorrow, the moment they're open, I'll hire a car.'

He pauses, shaking his head.

'Listen, Ian. That wasn't what I meant by talking.'

Ian interrogates him with his eyes.

'The answer,' says Dad, 'is yes.'

The confusion lingers in Ian's face.

'The question you asked me at the lock-up. You were right, Ian. I did kill a man.'

With that, Dad starts to talk. It's like a dam breaking. He tells Ian everything – about the oath, about Lou's peeler and the baby, about the hit, about Tina's death. All the while he is speaking he stares straight ahead, his story coming out in a kind of bruised and tortured monotone, as if he has taken his emotions and squeezed them dry. If he did it any other way, if he tried to tell Ian what it all meant to him, he would break down altogether. So what Ian hears is facts – hard, undeniable facts. They hit him like a boxer's combination punches: jabs, uppercuts, but, as yet, no KO. The only time Dad pauses is when he hears something outside. It happens twice. Each time he goes to check but comes back none the wiser.

'Something wrong?' Ian asks.

Dad shrugs but his gaze keeps darting to the window. It's obvious that, even here, they aren't safe.

'Maybe it would have been better to talk to the police,' Ian says when Dad is finished. 'You know, do your time, get it over with. It would have been history by now.'

Dad shakes his head.

'It doesn't work like that, son.'

'So tell me,' Ian says. 'How does it work?'

'You can't talk about the police force in Belfast the way you do here. In Northern Ireland, the rules are different. It's a war. You have fifth columns, traitors, spies. The Defenders – they had their eyes and ears in the police force. When you go to the peelers, you can never be quite sure who you're talking to.'

'Isn't there anybody you can trust?' Ian asks.

He imagines the life Dad lived in Belfast. It must have been like standing on a glass floor while it slowly cracked underneath him.

'There was one man,' says Dad. 'Ronnie Hagan. We were at school together. He was a prefect when I was a second year. Hard as nails, but straight, so far as I could tell. I actually thought about going to him once.'

He smiles at a memory.

'Funny thing about Hagan, his face was odd. I don't know what it was – a childhood accident maybe. He actually was two-faced. Physically, I mean. But, looking back, he's the only man I could have trusted.'

'But you didn't?'

'How could I? I only had one thing on my mind. I didn't want you growing up in those streets. There would always have been somebody like Chubby, drawing you in, trying to make you like him.'

Dad sucks in a breath.

'I made my decision.'

He fixes Ian with a stare.

'And don't think I don't regret it.'

He closes his eyes.

'Look, I know you blame me for your mum's death. We're together on that. I blame myself. I killed a Provo, drew their fire down on my family. You know, I can still hear McCullough in that bedroom, saying my name, giving me away. Chubby wanted to go back and kill McCann's wife too, just to shut her up. At least I stopped that happening.'

He meets Ian's stare, accepting the blame.

'I got away with my crimes, but don't believe I haven't done my time, son. Sure, I didn't go to prison, but since I left the North, what kind of a life have I had? There hasn't been a woman since your mum. I work, I raise my son. That's all I do. Whatever you think of me, you're my whole life.'

Ian listens. This is about the longest speech Dad has ever made, and he isn't finished yet.

'Living without friends, without a girlfriend or a wife, no career, no workmates, moving from place to place, living in fear, most of all living with guilt – you know what that is? It's doing time.'

He taps his forehead.

'This is my cell. The bars, the punishment block, the lock that turns at night – they're all here, in my head. If that isn't doing time, I don't know what is.'

Ian stares. Finally he says the only thing that comes to mind.

'Sorry, Dad.'

Dad puts a hand on Ian's shoulders.

'We're both tired, son. It's time to get your head down.'

He leads the way upstairs. There is a folding bed and mattress with a single sleeping bag. A baseball bat is standing against the wall. Dad sees Ian looking at the bat.

'That's for you,' he says. 'In case they find us.'

Ian nods grimly.

'Let's hope it doesn't come to that.'

Dad takes a pole with a hooked end from a wall cupboard. It's like the ones they use at school to open the high windows. Without a word, he pulls down the attic ladder and climbs up it. He returns with the money bag.

'I'm keeping this with me,' he says. 'We might have to get out quick.'

Ian looks around.

'So where are you sleeping?'

'I'll be in the second bedroom,' says Dad, 'though I won't be doing any sleeping. The door faces the stairs. Best place if anybody tries to break in.'

'You don't think . . . ?'

'That they'll find us?' Dad says, finishing Ian's sentence. 'I doubt it, but we'd be stupid to ignore the possibility. Chubby's a lot of things, but he isn't daft. I've no way of knowing how long they've been in town, trying to track me down.'

Dad goes to the door. He starts to shut it.

'No,' says Ian. 'Leave it open.'

Taking his hand off the doorknob, Dad bids him goodnight.

'Get your head down, son. It's been one hell of a day.'

But Ian finds it hard to settle. He goes over to the curtainless window and looks out. He can see the dual carriageway and the retail park, their details visible and hazed with amber underneath the streetlights. His eyes fasten on the two rows of prefabricated units and the deserted car park.

Retail park.

Retail park!

Why does that . . . ? Then he has it. He can feel a presence in the night, something brutish, destructive.

'Dad,' he calls, his voice shaking, 'what's this road called?'

The night-thing is approaching, seeking out its prey.

'What road?'

'Here, where we're staying.'

'Clanton Drive. Why?'

Ian's skin starts to prickle all over. The thing is here.

'Because McClean mentioned it.'

Dad appears at the door, horror etched into his greyish features.

'It was after they grabbed me,' Ian explains. 'He said they'd found the house. It was in Clanton Drive.'

Dad's face is as pale as the moon in the sky outside.

'But how?'

Ian thinks for a moment, then it comes.

'There was something about a notebook.'

Dad's face clouds as he processes the information.

'Of course,' he says after a few moments. 'How could I have been so stupid?'

Ian stares back.

'I left my notebook in the van. It's where I keep a log of my jobs. This address, Ian – it was in the notebook. They know where we are.'

Twenty-Eight

Was it Peter Moore or Kenny Kincaid who stood at the rail of the ferry, watching Belfast appear through the mist? It was hard to know. It was definitely Kenny Kincaid who had left this waterfront years earlier. But Kincaid had been doing his time. With the exception of his young son, who he was bringing up strong and decent, he'd had nobody to share his problems with, nobody to laugh and cry with. He had been solitary. One man alone with his past.

He had done his time.

But Tina Kincaid would have been proud of the man her Kenny had become. Peter Moore was as honest as they come, straight as a die. He never short-changed any of his customers. The work he did was first class, and always worth more than the price he charged. There was no better father either. His son was polite and well-mannered at school, a good student despite all the moving around. More importantly, he was considerate and purposeful. 'A lovely lad' – that was what all his teachers said.

But there was no avoiding it, the good father was still Kenny Kincaid. He might have done his time. He might have lived a better life, and in every way risen from the flames. He might have become a craftsman, with his own *life and his son's as his work. But the bloodstain was still there. The oath too. You can take the man out of Belfast, but you can't take Belfast out of the man.*

With every lapping wave, with every burst of seaspray, Kenny Kincaid was coming back home, if only for this weekend. He remembered the phone call. It had been his only connection with his past – a call once a month to Lou. He didn't tell her where he was. That way, nobody could get it out of her.

'How are they? How's Da? How's Ma?' he had asked.

But there had been silence on the line.

'Lou?'

'I'm so sorry, Kenny. It's Ma – she died last night. I was trying to make up my mind how to break it to you.'

So Kenny Kincaid decided to go home for the funeral. It was a risk, but this was his ma. He knew from Lou that Chubby and Billy were away in the Maze prison. Two of the old gang were off the streets. That just left Hughie McCullough. He was dangerous, but he was no Chubby Barr.

It was a risk Kenny had to take.

So he had agreed that Ian could go away for the weekend with Gareth Evans to the family's caravan in Pwhelli. Ian's eyes had been bigger and rounder than breakfast bowls. Could this really be true? Dad was letting him go away with friends! Kenny Kincaid smiled as he recalled the look of delight and surprise on Ian's face.

Then he saw the Belfast skyline becoming distinct and recognisable through the murk and the smile faded from his face.

Lou picked him up and they drove out through Antrim to an expanse of high moorland where Dad had brought them for walks when they were kids. There were farm buildings of whitewashed stone, scattered like pebbles among the heavy, dark green of the moors. Sheep grazed all around.

'You're looking well, Kenny,' Lou said.

'You too,' said Kenny.

'You know that's not true, Kenny,' she said. 'My life finished when they took my family.'

She let the thought hang before continuing.

'The rest is just killing time.'

Kenny didn't know what to say. He chose to change the subject.

'How's Peter?'

Peter was her second husband. They had married three years ago. He was a solid man by all accounts, and he loved Lou dearly. But he wasn't Andy. Lou was fond of Peter. She didn't love him.

'He's a good man,' Lou said. 'He deserves better than me.'

For the second time Kenny was stumped for a reply. He felt as if he were wading through the flotsam and jetsam of a distant shipwreck. But this debris had faces, voices. Pain washed in with it.

'How's Ian?' Lou asked.

'He's a great lad,' Kenny told her. 'He's gone away to Wales with a friend.'

'I'd love to see him.'

'Maybe you will,' Kenny said, 'one day.'

But they both knew that 'one day' was a long way off – as far away as the happiness that lay behind them.

'Do you really want to do this?' Lou asked. 'The funeral, I mean. They'll be looking out for you.'

'Not the peelers,' Kenny said. 'They're bound to keep a watching brief, but they've got no evidence – not about the money, not about Joe McCann. The law won't touch me.'

Lou winced at the mention of the man who had destroyed her family.

'They've got nothing on me.'

'The Defenders then?'

Kenny shook his head.

'I don't think so. Since Chubby and the boys chose to go freelance with the Portadown raid, the Defenders have washed their hands of the lot of us. They've bigger fish to fry these days, what with the peace process and all. It's me against Chubby, Billy and Hugh – that's the top and bottom of it. Hughie McCullough's the only one on the streets just now. He doesn't worry me.'

Lou shuddered.

'He worries me.'

Kenny took Lou's arm and they walked together, wishing the years could fade and their golden days return.

Twenty-Nine

'Do you think we should get out?' Ian asks.

He looks at Dad, who gestures weakly, almost in despair.

'I don't know,' he whispers. 'I don't know.'

'Maybe if we go now, we can get away before they come . . .'

Dad's look slashes across the darkened room and rests on Ian.

'For God's sake!' he barks. 'Just let me think.'

But he can't think. That much is obvious to Ian. He doesn't even feel angry about being shouted at. He knows the strain Dad is under. The thought of the three men, out there in the darkness, approaching the house, is paralysing him. He has taken a few measures – killing the lights, hauling a cupboard to the top of the stairs to act as a makeshift barricade. There is little purpose in the activity, however. He is doing it for show, proof that he hasn't given up. But at least one part of him seems to think they are finished.

'Why don't we just give them the money?' Ian suggests after a few moments' silence.

Dad's head sags.

'It wouldn't do much good,' he says. 'They're not just after the money.'

Immediately understanding what Dad is telling him, what he tried to tell him all those hours earlier, Ian gives a brief nod and looks out of the window at the amber lights of the retail park, the trees threshing in the damp darkness, the unknown shapes between.

'They could be out there right now.'

'Which is a good reason to stay put. I'm sorry for all this, son. If I could only turn the clock back . . .'

'Forget it,' Ian tells him. 'What's done is done.'

Neither of them speaks for a while. They sit in the empty room with the blackness drawn around them like a blanket. Then Dad's mobile rings. He glances at the number and cancels it.

'Who was that?' Ian asks.

'Nobody,' Dad replies.

'But if it's–'

'I said nobody!'

His voice softens.

'Get your head down if you can, son,' he says.

Ian shakes his head.

'I'm OK, Dad.'

Sleep is the last thing on his mind.

'It's no use,' says Lomas. 'He's not answering his phone.'

Hagan punches the dashboard.

'You're a damned fool, Kenny!' he says, cursing. 'What do you think's going to happen if they get to you first?'

He stares out of the window at the night-time streets.

'Try phoning the station again,' he says. 'There were a couple of leads you were chasing up.'

Lomas nods.

'And?'

'Nothing.'

Ian blinks away the gloom. There is a sour taste in his mouth.

'Have I been asleep?'

'Yes,' says Dad. 'A few hours.'

'What time is it?'

'Three o'clock.'

'Three!'

Ian looks around.

'Is there anything to drink?'

'Can of Coke in the bag. There's a sandwich too if you want it.'

That's when Ian realises just how hungry he is. He has hardly eaten since ten o'clock this – yesterday – morning. Two rounds of toast that Vicky made him, that's it. In books the heroes never seem to eat, and in a crisis they can't eat. But Ian eats – ravenously, stuffing every bit of the sandwich into his mouth before washing it down with the Coke. Normally he wouldn't drink it unless chilled. Now he just doesn't care.

'When do you think they'll come?' he asks.

'They're probably here,' says Dad. 'Waiting.'

'But when will they come in?'

'If I know Chubby, any time now.'

He explains Chubby's routine.

'Between three and four, that's when he makes his move. He read about it somewhere – the way men are at their lowest ebb in the early hours.'

Dad stops.

'Do you really want to hear this, Ian?'

'Yes.'

'There will be one man in the car – Billy. He's the driver.

His job is to get the boys away. Chubby, he'll sledge-hammer the door. As for McCullough . . .'

His eyes turn towards the darkened stairwell.

'He'll be first up the stairs.'

Ian imagines the attack. Two dark figures pounding up the stairs, McCullough in front, Barr coming up behind. That's when he has second thoughts.

'It might not be McCullough,' he says.

'Come again?'

Ian explains about the comb.

'Anything else?'

'Well, McClean hurt his wrist. You know about that.'

'Two men hurt,' says Dad thoughtfully. 'Maybe that evens things up a bit.'

But not enough.

Thirty

It rained the day of the funeral.

To begin with, Kenny stood some distance from the mourners, running his eyes over those present. Lou knew he was coming, of course. Da too. They didn't tell anyone else, even family. Just in case. Kenny's older brother Robert would be as surprised as anyone that he had come. Still, there was no Hugh McCullough. No prying eyes sent by the Defenders. Nobody he need worry about.

Eventually, after some minutes' observation, Kenny started the slow walk between the leaning tombstones, taking his time over the rain-slicked grass. Though he had his coat collar pulled up and walked with his head hunched he was recognised immediately. A buzz of whispers greeted his arrival. Everyone recognised the newcomer. He had changed, of course. Who wouldn't in almost ten years? His hair, plastered down by the driving rain, was greying slightly at the temples. He seemed to have lost a little weight, too. But what everybody noticed was Kenny's eyes. They seemed haunted, the brightness all drained out of them by Tina's death and the strains of the ensuing years.

Though Kenny knew that everyone was staring at him, he did nothing to acknowledge their looks. He stared straight ahead instead, watching the age-old ritual, listening to the words that were so familiar they had become the stuff of satire.

'Forasmuch as it hath pleased Almighty God of His great mercy to take unto Himself the soul of our dear sister here departed, we therefore commit her body to the ground.'

Kenny felt Lou's arm link his. He turned and gave a grim smile. Nodding briefly to her husband Peter, he turned back to the grave.

'Earth to earth; ashes to ashes; dust to dust.'

Then there was only the scrape of tossed soil on the coffin lid and the drumming of the rain on earth and on polished wood. When it was all over Kenny watched the mourners moving away towards their cars. Nobody came near him, not even his uncles and aunts. Then, for the first time, somebody spoke.

'Welcome home, Kenny.'

It was Hugh McCullough.

Hugh didn't believe in small talk. His second sentence went straight to the point.

'You've got some neck coming back here, Kenny. We've been looking for you for a long time.'

Kenny looked around theatrically.

'What do you mean "we"? You're the only one I can see, Hughie.' He forced a chuckle. 'Oh yes, I forgot. Your little playmates are away in the Maze, aren't they? What was it they did – take a little girl's daddy from her? Big men. The Maze should suit them. A real class establishment, so I hear. Five-star accommodation throughout.'

At the mention of the Maze prison, McCullough scowled. He'd had a spell in there himself.

'Don't try to act superior,' McCullough said. 'You took a little girl's daddy too.'

Kenny lowered his head.

'Yes, I did.'

'You cost us a fortune,' McCullough said. 'A quarter of a mill, split four ways – that's what we were talking about, Kenny boy. But you had to be greedy and have it all to yourself. So what did you do with it?'

Kenny hesitated just long enough to make McCullough think. He could feel the man's hard eyes boring into him. Then the eyes narrowed.

'You've still got it, haven't you?'

McCullough held his breath for a beat, waiting for Kenny to contradict him, then he laughed out loud.

'I don't believe it! You could have spent the lot. You're really something, Kenny. All that money and you don't touch a penny.'

'I wouldn't go that far. I spent some.'

'Some,' said McCullough, 'but not all. How much is left – half? Three-quarters? No, I know, you're not going to tell me. It's still a cool little fortune though, isn't it?'

Kenny wanted to get hold of McCullough and slap the smile from his face, but it was his ma's funeral.

'Oh, I got you all wrong, didn't I?' McCullough continued. 'What was it stopped you, Kenny? Principles? Yes, you were always big on principles. You never wanted to have fun, you just wanted to fight the war, show the Fenians who was boss.'

'Nobody's boss,' Kenny said, interrupting. 'Prod or Taig, we're all victims.'

McCullough wasn't listening.

'Is that it then?' he asked, beating the same drum. 'Your principles got in the way? Or were you just plain scared?'

Kenny regretted his mistake, allowing McCullough to guess most of the money was still intact, but it didn't really matter. Whether he had the money or not, he was a dead man walking. Had been since he walked away with it in the first place.

'Scared of you, McCullough?' Kenny snarled. 'Don't flatter yourself.'

McCullough blinked the raindrops out of his eyes. He was bareheaded and the rain was sluicing over his hairless skull.

'I'll tell you what, Kenny boy. Funeral or no funeral, you made a mistake coming back here. We spent years trying to track you down. Just missed you a couple of times, then Chubby and Billy got put away and I had to put things on hold. Sure we wanted revenge, but we wanted the money more, and we thought you must have spent it all. What man wouldn't?'

He gripped Kenny's sleeve.

'Don't you get too comfy over there, because we're going to be after you. It's a great thing, the peace process. Chubby and Billy will be out in a couple of months. That's right – the boys are back in town. This time we'll find you. We want our money.'

Kenny looked deep into McCullough's eyes and read the dark promise in them. He was a dead man walking all right. He shrugged his hand away.

'You know what?' he said. 'You're sick, McCullough.'

McCullough laughed.

'And you, Kenny,' he said, 'you're scared.'

Kenny spun round on his heel and walked away briskly. He imagined Barr and McClean walking out of the Maze.

The worst thing about what McCullough had said: it was true.

Kenny lost McCullough just south of Liverpool. The skull-headed man had sat just a few yards from him all the way over on the ferry. For all the close attention on the return

166

journey, it didn't give Kenny much pleasure, losing his pursuer. No matter how hard he tried, he was positive that, sooner or later, they would come knocking at his door. All he was doing was delaying the inevitable. Still, it was worth doing. Sure, Kenny wasn't going to make it easy for the boys to find him. Plus there was always the chance that they were dimmer than he gave them credit for. So he did what he had to. He paid all his fares in cash, left false names. Anyone following Kenny Kincaid would have been continually put off the scent by a trail of false names, fake addresses and pre-planned red herrings. As he made his way round Merseyside and through Cheshire he double-, then triple-checked that McCullough had been left far behind. He pulled in at two sets of Services, one in completely the opposite direction to home, sitting in a corner of the restaurant and watching the comings and goings. He parked, again in a corner of the car park, and watched the new arrivals for several minutes before pulling away and rejoining the motorway.

Only when he was absolutely certain that he was in the clear did Kenny Kincaid strike out for home and reunion with Ian. As he turned into Rochester Avenue to await Ian's return from Pwhelli, he sloughed off his former identity. From now on he would only answer to the name Peter Moore.

Thirty-One

Four o'clock has come and gone. It is nearly a quarter past already and the house's quiet security remains unbreached. But out in the sighing night three men are waiting. There have been showers all night and now a downpour has started. Fat, cold drops of rain thud against the window panes. Ian glances, first at his father, then down the gloomy stairwell. He imagines the attack: how they will smash into the house, how they will storm the stairs, finally, what they will do if they get past Dad's makeshift barricade.

'They're late,' Ian says, breaking the uneasy silence.

He even dares hope the injuries to McCullough and McClean are worse than he'd thought – that they are out of action.

'They'll come,' Dad says.

Ian doesn't know if it's the right thing to say, but he speaks his mind anyway.

'I'm scared.'

And from Dad, no attempt at bravado.

'Me too.'

By way of proof, Dad holds his hand out. Even in the darkened landing Ian can see his fingers quivering.

'Some people don't seem to show fear,' Dad says. 'Chubby's like that. He doesn't seem to think about things. It's like animal instinct. He just acts. I don't think I've ever seen him hesitate.'

'Do you admire that?' Ian asks.

'Are you kidding?' Dad retorts. 'Animal instinct is just that – *animal*. I hate it. The worst choices I ever made in my life were because I tried to be like him. When I joined the Defenders, I was taking a ride on a runaway train. I should have got off while I still could.'

Then a nervous afterthought.

'Things could have been good for me, son. You, me and your mother. For keeps.'

Fleetingly, his face is swept by an expression of sheer joy, as if picturing the scene in his mind could make it come true.

'Imagine that, Ian boy. Things could have been good.'

Listening to his father's words, Ian wants to make peace.

'They have been good, Dad.'

'That's not what you said earlier on.'

'It's true though,' Ian insists. 'Remember you said you've been doing time in your head?'

Dad nods.

'All that time you were feeling bad, I never even knew. I was too busy having a happy childhood. So we had to move a few times? Big deal. It never did me any harm.'

Ian wonders if he's laying it on a bit thick.

'You must think I'm a real spoilt brat. I've been really selfish, haven't I?'

'No, you were being a kid, that's all. I had no right to take your childhood.'

Then a change comes over him, as though he has heard his own words and made a decision. He fumbles in his pocket.

'What are you doing?' Ian asks.

Dad takes out his mobile.

'Something I should have done hours ago.'

Hagan and Lomas are back in the police station. Lomas is sitting at his desk. His head is hanging so low Hagan can't even see his face.

'You can go home, you know,' says Hagan. 'No reason to stay. There are other officers on duty.'

'I'll see it through,' says Lomas.

The phone rings. He takes the call and looks at Hagan.

'It's Kincaid.'

Hagan takes the phone. 'You've made the right choice, Kenny.'

He puts the phone down.

'The Armed Response Unit?' he asks.

'Standing by.'

Hagan takes his coat from the peg.

'Tell them we're moving.'

'Are you sure about this?' Ian asks.

Dad nods.

'I'm a damned fool for not doing it earlier. How was I supposed to defend you from three of them?'

Ian moves away from the window, crouching low.

'What are you doing?' Dad asks.

'Folding up the camp bed.'

'Why?'

Ian pulls the bed into the corner, nudges off the mattress and folds the frame. 'Just giving myself something to do. It's not like I'm going to get any more sleep.'

He shoves the mattress and the frame against the wall under the window.

'This mattress is a bit big for a camp bed, isn't it?'

Dad shrugs.

'It was in one of the rooms. The last owners must have left it. I wanted you to be comfortable.'

He thinks for a moment.

'Makes a lot of sense, doesn't it? I expose you to three psychopaths and I'm worried about the mattress being too thin. A bit rich, don't you think?'

They are still laughing about the mattress and the psychos when the kitchen window bursts in a storm of broken glass. Moments later there is the sound of the door jamb splintering open. Dad's voice snaps through the early morning murk.

'They're here.'

Hagan and Lomas are in the third car. The two vans of the Armed Response Unit lead the convoy. Lomas speaks first.

'I wonder what made him change his mind.'

Hagan shrugs.

'Maybe he's tired. He's sick of running.'

Lomas watches the sleeping town flashing by.

'One thing I still don't understand,' he says.

'What's that?'

'The soft spot you've got for this Kenny Kincaid.'

He sees a protest forming.

'And don't try to tell me you haven't. I've only got to listen to you talk. I mean, he's a gunman, you've said so yourself. Come on, what gives?'

The ghost of a smile crosses Hagan's asymmetric features.

'I have taken a special interest in Kenny,' he admits. 'There's a bit of a connection, you see.'

'You're related to him?'

'No, nothing like that. I knew him at school. He was in the second or third year as I was about to leave.'

'That's a bit of an age difference. What makes you remember him?'

'You don't forget somebody like Kenny. He was a strange combination – bright but trouble. I was a prefect that year. One time the teachers told us some younger boys were messing in the corridors. We were to throw them out. Kenny was one of them.'

'What happened?'

'The others went without a murmur. Not Kenny. He fought like a wildcat. He was only thirteen but it took three of us to shift him. He took a right beating.'

'Why didn't he just go?'

Hagan chuckles.

'I asked him that later.'

'And?'

'We didn't say please. Kenny's like that. He stands on principle.'

'It sounds like you're making excuses for him, Mr Hagan.'

'Excuses? No, that's not it. But I was intrigued. For a boy to have so much promise and throw it all away – I wanted to know why. I suppose I could see something of myself in him. A few years later I got my chance to get to know Kenny at first hand. I started to come across him in the course of my job. It was kids' stuff at first, then he started to get drawn in deeper.'

'So you followed his . . . career?'

'Yes. In a way, Kenny's life is the story of the Troubles. There are plenty like him on both sides of the barricades – good men made mad.'

Hagan glances at Lomas.

'And don't go telling me I'm making excuses, son. What do you think caused all the violence? Something in the water? No, we're ordinary folk who are victims of our history. This is fact I'm telling you – God's honest truth. The gunmen who've fought this war, they're not monsters. There's a man behind the gun.'

Hagan punches home his point.

'And a child behind the man. Somewhere along the way the child gets lost.'

'You mean you could have turned out the same?'

'Given the right circumstances, why not? So could you, if you'd been brought up over the water. There but for fortune, son.'

Lomas sees the retail park coming up on the left. Hagan's words run through his mind.

There but for fortune.

When the attack comes, it comes fast, with the thunder of running feet on uncarpeted floors, the appearance of two dark shapes at the bottom of the stairs, finally with the explosion of a gun in the narrow stairwell and a cascade of plaster and painted woodwork. Ian has heard gunshots before – hundreds, thousands of them in countless movies and TV dramas. But nothing has prepared him for this – the deafening report that fills the air and cannons round your skull. In almost the same split-second that the gun goes off – whose, Ian can't tell – Dad is yelling at him.

'Get down! Stay down!'

A figure is halfway up the stairs, roughly silhouetted against the half-light of streetlamps cast through the down-stairs windows.

'Stop right there, Billy! So help me, I'll fire!'

McClean doesn't stop but there is something odd about his approach. Then Ian understands. He is a right-handed man holding a gun in his left. Ian sees Dad take aim and fire. A shriek of pain detonates through the crazed black-ness. Ian can make out the wolfman clutching his thigh. It's obvious to Ian that Dad fired low deliberately. He knows what killing a man feels like. He doesn't want to do it again. But the attack isn't over. Another figure clambers over his groaning comrade. Another explosion rips open the fabric of the night. It's Dad's turn to cry out.

'Dad!'

Ian reaches for his father but his hand is shrugged away. Dad gets off a shot with a shaking hand. Barr ducks down but he hasn't been hit. He watches with satisfaction as Dad's trembling fingers lose their grip on the gun.

Barr steps forward to finish the job.

At the sound of shots Lomas and Hagan exchange glances.

'Sounds like it's going down,' says Lomas.

There's a quiver in his voice. This isn't the kind of incident he's used to in his quiet little town. Hagan doesn't reply. He is already on the radio, talking to the Armed Response Unit's officer-in-charge.

'Deploy your men immediately,' he said. 'If my information is correct, we've got four men, four firearms being used. Almost certainly we've got a fourteen-year-old boy in the house.'

But as the vehicles screech to a halt there is the sound of shattering glass. An upstairs window has blown out, followed by a body.

Barr is standing over Dad. He is panting.

'So where's the money, Kenny boy?'

Dad is holding his side. Ian can see blood seeping between his fingers – thick, dark streams, separating, spreading. For all the pain etched on his face, Dad still manages a show of defiance.

'Find it yourself, Chubby.'

Dad's gun is on the second stair. Barr kicks it out of reach.

'Oh, I will, believe me.'

Straightening up, Chubby points the gun barrel at Kenny's head.

'I'll count to three.'

Ian doesn't count that far. Grabbing the baseball bat, he swings it. He hears the crack as it crunches into Barr's shoulder joint. Tears running down his face, Ian swings again. He hears the oddest sound.

Clunk!

It's almost funny, but he knows what it is. Bone. The bat has caught Barr on the skull.

He goes down.

Even then the nightmare isn't over. Barr is slumped against the wall, semi-conscious, but McClean is hobbling up the stairs. Behind him McCullough has entered the house and is already climbing.

'Dad!' Ian cries. 'Are you all right? Can you move?'

Dad nods.

'But there's nowhere to go, son.'

Ian knows different. Grabbing the frame of the camp bed, he hurls it through the window. Snatching a glance at McClean's lumbering form, he starts shoving the mattress through the window.

'Give me a hand!' he yells.

Normal time crumples. Events occur like camera shots, the sequence too fast to order. Dad is at his side, shoving desperately at the mattress. McClean is at the top of the landing, gun in hand. McCullough is coming up behind.

'Go!' Ian screams, seeing the injured McClean struggling to aim his revolver. 'I'll follow you out.'

In the same split second three things happen: the mattress hits the ground outside, Dad tumbles through the window, blood spitting out between his fingers; Ian follows him out.

In the next split second there is an exchange of shouts, then another gunshot and a cry. A life has ended.

Hagan is in the house when the last shot is fired.

'Who's down?' he demands.

He is striding forward, moving into the confusion.

'I said: who's down?'

As he makes his way upstairs, he sees McCullough spreadeagled against the wall. Armed officers still have their weapons trained on him. Barr is also propped against a wall, waiting for medical attention. Hagan asks his question again.

'Will somebody speak to me? I know a man is down. Who is it?'

That's when he sees the wolfman, lifeless eyes staring at the ceiling.

'McClean.'

The officer in charge approaches Hagan.

'A warning was given,' he explains. 'The gunman refused to put down his weapon. There was no alternative.'

'For God's sake, man, I'm not questioning what you did! I'm trying to find Kincaid.'

That's when he hears Lomas's voice outside.

'Stop!'

Kenny doesn't stop. With his hands still clamped to his side, sticky and glued with blood, with his knee burning with pain where he landed half-on, half-off the mattress, he stumbles forward.

'Stop!'

Ian catches up with Dad. He grabs his arm.

'Where are you going?' he asks. 'What do you think you're doing?'

'I'm not going to prison. I can't.'

'Dad, don't be stupid! You can't get away.'

Kenny stops. Ian said *you*. Not us, but you. His son has accepted that the long adventure has come to an end. Eleven years of running are over. There is no Peter Moore now. Chubby Barr was right all along. The oath was forever, but not the way Chubby meant. Kenny Kincaid took it. He sold his soul. Now he is suffering the consequences.

Somebody shouts.

'Raise your hands. Put them behind your head. Now lie face down on the ground.'

Ian nods, his eyes pleading with Dad. But Dad has one more question.

'The money?' he asks.

'Forget it,' Ian tells him. 'I left it in the house. It didn't seem important.'

'You're right,' Kenny laughs. 'It isn't.'

Then he does as he's told, lying down on the rain-washed ground.

Ten minutes later Ian is sitting in an ambulance opposite his father. Kenny Kincaid is sitting on a gurney. He has a blanket round his shoulders and a female paramedic is putting a temporary dressing on the graze to his ribcage. Red and blue lights flash round them.

'You're lucky,' she says. 'It looks like superficial tissue damage.'

'A flesh wound,' Ian says.

The paramedic laughs.

'You've been watching too much TV.'

Then Hagan's lopsided face appears at the ambulance doors and the laughter stops. The paramedic makes herself scarce.

'So are you going to talk to us now, Kenny?'

Ian stares in disbelief at what Dad says next.

'I'm no tout, Mr Hagan.'

'I didn't say you were, Kenny.'

'Is there any way I can stay out of prison?' Kenny asks. He glances at Ian. 'I've got my boy to bring up.'

Ian looks hopefully at Hagan. You can't do it, his eyes plead. You can't send him to prison.

'Depends what you've got to say to me,' Hagan tells him.

Ian's heart fills with hope. Say something, Dad – anything. You can't throw away your freedom.

Kenny lowers his voice.

'If I talk about the boys – Chubby, Billy, Hugh – can we cut a deal about that?'

Hagan sighs.

'There isn't much we can do about Billy McClean. He's dead.'

Ian's mind fills with an image of the wolfman pawing at him through the concertina doors of the lift.

'Jeez!'

'Look, Kenny,' says Hagan, 'we've got the money. We've got Barr and McCullough. If I'm going to keep you out of prison, I need a lot more than that. I need the men at the top: names, dates, history. Come on, Kenny – you don't owe these people anything.'

Hearing this, Kenny gives his head a long, sad shake.

Ian stares at Dad.

'What are you saying?'

But Dad isn't listening.

'Is that your last word, Mr Hagan? No deal unless I tell you everything?'

'Tell him, Dad,' says Ian. 'Tell him anything he wants to know. You walked away from all those people. They don't mean anything to you now. Why are you defending them?'

But Dad has made his decision.

'I'll talk about the boys – Chubby, Billy and Hugh – and that's all.'

'No good, Kenny,' says Hagan. 'Helping us build a case against Barr and McCullough might help, but it won't keep you out of prison. For that, I need the Defenders, the main players. I need it all.'

'The politicians won't let you move against the Defenders,' Kenny says. 'Some of them have gone *respectable*.'

He spits the word out, as if he's swearing.

'Maybe not,' says Hagan. 'That's not my choice. I give them the evidence. After that, it's in their court. I need you to give me the leadership of the organisation, Kenny.'

'Then I've more time to do, Mr Hagan,' Dad says. 'I'm no tout.'

'Your choice,' says Hagan, turning to go. 'It looks like we've nothing else to talk about.'

'Please,' says Ian, 'don't go! Dad's done his time. Eleven years. This isn't justice!'

Then, like the little boy he used to be, he cries: 'It isn't fair!'

There is a veil of tears in front of his eyes as he watches Hagan walk away.

Thirty-Two

Three people get out of the car and stretch their legs. They are at a place called World's End, high above the north Wales town of Llangollen. Two of the group are middle-aged, the third is in his late teens. A fourth person remains staring straight ahead in the passenger seat, as if waiting to become acclimatised to the brave new world outside the metal shell.

'Are you coming?' says the woman.

She is in her mid-forties. There was a time in her life, not so very long ago, when she looked much older, but those days have passed. She has known what it is like to go through the motions, to walk down all the long days while life happens to you. Then, one day out of the blue, she was needed. There was a boy alone, the way she was alone when she lost her husband and baby.

That was when Lou Flanagan, née Kincaid, found the strength to help somebody who needed her. It was the saving of her – being needed by this nephew she hadn't seen in eleven years. All that time she had known one way to survive and that was to close up, seal off all entries to her heart, cauterise her feelings against the world outside. And she had done it – she had survived. But Ian had needed more than a woman who breathed, cooked, tidied, existed.

He had needed a family.

In Lou and Peter Flanagan he had got just that.

Peter had a good job in the civil service. It wasn't difficult to transfer to England. It was much harder to make a home. They were strangers at first, Lou, Peter and Ian, but they grew into each other. They set up house only a couple of miles from Rochester Avenue. Ian was thrilled to discover it was only five minutes' walk from Hunger Hill and Vicky Shaw.

Fish out of water at first, Lou and Peter found a purpose in rebuilding Ian's broken life. And what they did to put his life back together, they did well. Four years ago they had started the job and now, on the day of the A-level results, it is almost finished. The boy is on the brink of manhood.

'Are we going for this walk, or what?' Ian says.

'That depends on your dad,' Lou tells him.

She crouches down by the open window.

'Are you ready, Kenny?' she asks.

It takes a moment for Kenny Kincaid to shift his gaze from the hills and focus on his sister's face.

'It's so beautiful,' he says, looking at the sunlit slopes. 'You too.'

His words bring back memories. This time he is telling the truth. Lou Kincaid, who has looked sixty, is forty-five but could pass for thirty-five. Kenny clambers out of the passenger seat and stands up.

'Thanks for taking care of Ian, Lou. You've done a good job.'

'I'm not the only one,' she says, linking her arm through Kenny's. 'He's brought me back to life, that boy of yours.'

It's true. After all this time she has even let Peter in. She has learned to love again.

Leaning against Kenny, she pulls a handkerchief out of her sleeve and dabs at her eyes.

'So much wasted time.'

Kenny shakes his head.

'Life's never completely wasted,' he says, 'even when you suffer.'

'Aren't we getting philosophical?' Lou says. 'I've got a thought for you, too. Love is like buses. Years without any, then it all comes along at once. It's almost too much to bear.'

Kenny nods. He knows what she means. This morning he walked out of prison after serving four years of his sentence. He did what he had to. He stayed out of trouble. He got some qualifications. He knew that one day he would have his life back. That single thought was enough to keep him alive. This morning he walked free. Now he is strolling on a Welsh hillside.

Almost too much to bear.

'He'll be on his travels soon,' says Kenny, indicating Ian.

Lou smiles.

'Yes, he's off in two weeks – the grand European tour. He's got his backpack ready.'

She calls Ian over.

'Haven't you got some news for your da?' she says.

Ian grins.

'I got two As and a B, Dad. I start at Liverpool University in October.'

Kenny rests a hand on Ian's shoulders.

'Nice one, son. Got any plans for when you graduate?'

'Dunno,' says Ian. 'Teaching maybe. I can take my time deciding. It's three years off.'

He winks.

'I intend to enjoy myself first.'

He looks fidgety.

'Something wrong?' asks Kenny.

'I need to phone Vicky,' says Ian. 'See how she's done. I missed her at school, you know, what with meeting you out of prison.'

'Don't mind me,' says Kenny. 'Give the girl a call.'

Ian takes a walk to an exposed crag.

'She showed a lot of strength, that girl of his,' says Lou. 'Two years her parents tried to stop her seeing Ian. The Shaws did everything to poison Vicky against him.'

'I know,' says Kenny. 'The boy's had it tough.'

They watch Ian talking. He's back a couple of minutes later, a broad beam on his face.

'Guess what? She's in.'

'So where's Vicky going?' Kenny asks.

'Oh, come on,' Lou says. 'Work it out for yourself.'

'Liverpool?'

Ian winks.

'Got it in one.'

'Let's take that walk,' says Kenny. 'I've a lot of living to do.'

So they walk on, Lou and Peter, Ian and Kenny. They don't speak. They don't need to. All that needs to be said has been said. As for what remains unspoken, maybe there are no words for that. But there is something they all know.

The dead don't come back to life. Lost years can't be returned.

Time doesn't take away the pain.

But it can heal.

Also by Alan Gibbons

The Edge

Danny is a boy on the edge. A boy teetering on the brink of no return, living in fear.

Cathy is his mother. She's been broken by fear.

Chris Kane is fear – and they belong to him.

But one day they escape. They're looking for freedom, for the promised land where they can start really living. Instead they find prejudice, and danger of another kind.

Uncompromising and disturbing, but utterly readable, Alan Gibbons' latest novel positively crackles with tension as he writes about a mother and her son desperate to start a new life.

Shortlisted for the Carnegie Medal.

The Dark Beneath

'Today I shot the girl I love.'

GCSEs are over and sixteen-year-old Imogen is looking forward to a perfect, lazy English summer. But her world is turned upside down by three refugees, all hiding from life. Anthony is fourteen, already an outcast, bullied and shunned by his peers. Farid is an asylum seeker from Afghanistan, who has travelled across continents seeking peace. And Gordon Craig is a bitter, lonely man. She knows all of them, but she doesn't know how dangerous they are. Being part of their lives could cost Imogen her own.

Supercharged with tension and drama, Alan Gibbons' novel is about what happens when the fabric of normality is ripped apart exposing the terrifying dark beneath.

Caught in the Crossfire

'You know what happens to people like you? You get hit in the crossfire.'

Shockwaves sweep the world in the aftermath of 11 September. The Patriotic League barely need an excuse in their fight to get Britain back for the British, but this is chillingly perfect.

Rabia and Tahir are British Muslims, Daz and Jason are out looking for trouble, Mike and Liam are brothers on different sides. None of them will escape unscarred from the terrifying and tragic events which will weave their lives together.

Marking a new dimension in his writing on race, riots and real life, *Caught in the Crossfire* is an unforgettable novel that Alan Gibbons needed to write.

'Gibbons' writing often addresses worrying issues of social justice but never as powerfully as in this novel . . . the writing – short, sharp pieces that take us into the mind of each character – is accessible and compulsive.'
Wendy Cooling, *The Bookseller*

The Lost Boys' Appreciation Society

Something was wrong. The anger-flash had drained out of Dad's face, replaced by a blank pallor.

Like disbelief . . .

When Mum was killed in a car crash our lives were wrecked too.

Gary, John and Dad are lost without Mum. Gary is only 14 and goes seriously off the rails, teetering on the brink of being on the wrong side of the law. John is wrestling with GCSEs and his first romance – but he's carrying the burden of trying to cope with Gary and Dad at the same time. And they're all living with the memories of someone they can never replace.

Alan Gibbons writes with compassion – and flashes of humour – about surviving against all the odds.

The Shadow of the Minotaur

'Real life' or the death defying adventures of the Greek myths, with their heroes and monsters, daring deeds and narrow escapes – which would you choose?

For Phoenix it's easy. He hates his new home and the new school where he is bullied. He's embarrassed by his computer geek dad. But when he logs on to the Legendeer, the game his dad is working on, he can be a hero. He is Theseus fighting the terrifying Minotaur, or Perseus battling with snake-haired Medusa.

The trouble is The Legendeer is more than just a game. Play it if you dare.

Vampyr Legion

What if there are real worlds where our nightmares live and wait for us?

Phoenix has found one and it's alive. Armies of bloodsucking vampyrs and terrifying werewolves, the creatures of our darkest dreams, are poised to invade our world.

But Phoenix has encountered the creator of *Vampyr Legion*, the evil Gamesmaster, before and knows that this deadly computer game is for real – he must win or never come back.

Warriors of the Raven

The game opens up the gateway between our world and the world of the myths.

The Gamesmaster almost has our world at his mercy. Twice before fourteen-year-old Phoenix has battled against him in *Shadow of the Minotaur* and *Vampyr Legion*, but Warriors of the Raven is the game at its most complex and deadly level. This time, Phoenix enters the arena for the final conflict, set in the world of Norse myth. Join Phoenix in Asgard to fight Loki, the Mischief-maker, the terrifying Valkyries, dragons and fire demons – and hope for victory. Our future depends on him.

Julie and Me . . . and Michael Owen Makes Three

It's been a year of own goals for Terry.

– Man U, the entire focus of his life (what else is there?), lose to arch-enemies Liverpool FC.

– he looks like Chris Evans, no pecs.

– Mum and Dad split up (just another statistic).

– he falls seriously in love with drop dead gorgeous Julie. It's bad enough watching Frisky Fitzy (school golden boy) drool all over her, but worse still she's an ardent Liverpool FC supporter.

Life as Terry knows it is about to change in this hilariously funny, sometimes sad, utterly readable modern Romeo and Juliet story.

Julie and Me: Treble Trouble

For one disastrous year Terry has watched Julie, the girl of his dreams, go out with arch rival Frisky Fitz, seen his Mum and Dad's marriage crumble and his beloved Man U go the same way. 2001 has got to be better.

– Will he get to run his hands through the lovely Julie's raven tresses?

– What happens when his new streamlined Mum gets a life?

– Can Man U redeem themselves and do the business in the face of the impossible?

Returning the love – that's what it's all about.

Read the concluding part of *Julie and Me* and all will be revealed.